SHIRLEE McCOY

Die Before Nightfall

Steeple Hill®

Published by Steeple Hill Books™

STEEPLE HILL BOOKS

Steeple
Hill®

ISBN 0-373-44221-1

DIE BEFORE NIGHTFALL

Copyright © 2005 by Shirlee McCoy

This edition published by arrangement with Steeple Hill Books.

® and TM are trademarks of Steeple Hill Books, used under license.
Trademarks indicated with ® are registered in the United States Patent
and Trademark Office, the Canadian Trade Marks Office and in other
countries.

www.SteepleHill.com

Printed in U.S.A.

"Running away, Raven?"

"Not running." Raven turned away. "Going home."

"What is it about me that makes you nervous?" Shane asked. Caught in the spell of sunset, Raven didn't realize Shane had moved until he was beside her, his hand clasping hers gently. "Stay for a little longer. I promise I won't talk about princes, frogs, or *you.*"

"No, it's getting dark. I'd better head home." Raven pulled her hand from his and moved through the overgrown cemetery, leading Merry along beside her. Already dusk was beginning to settle on the land, deep violet shadows creeping across the ground. The effect was eerie, the rustle of leaves and hum of insects only adding to Raven's unease.

Her foot caught on a root and she stumbled, barely catching her balance. A twig snapped somewhere to the right and Merry growled low in her throat, lunging toward the sound.

"Hello?"

No one answered, nothing moved in the darkness, yet Raven was sure someone was there. She didn't wait for more. Breath gasping, heart hammering, she raced toward the cottage.

Books by Shirlee McCoy

Steeple Hill Trade
Still Waters #4

Love Inspired Suspense
Die Before Nightfall #5

SHIRLEE McCOY

has always loved making up stories. As a child, she daydreamed elaborate tales in which she was the heroine—gutsy, strong and invincible. Though she soon grew out of her superhero fantasies, her love for storytelling never diminished. She knew early that she wanted to write inspirational fiction, and began writing her first novel when she was a teenager. Still, it wasn't until her third son was born that she truly began pursuing her dream of being published. Three years later she sold her first book. Now a busy mother of four, Shirlee is a homeschool mom by day and an inspirational author by night. She and her husband and children live in Maryland and share their house with a dog and a guinea pig.

Jude, Caleb, Seth and Emma Grace, if God lined up all the children in the world and let me choose any four, I would choose the four of you. And if you had dirty faces, messy clothes and were whining and crying, I would still choose you. I love you. All the way to the sun and back. Always. No matter what.

A special thank-you to Sara Parker, who read my first, second, third and fourth drafts without flinching, and who offered countless suggestions and advice. And to my editor, Krista Stroever, who walked me through the publication process with grace, humor and an unerring eye for detail. Thanks! This book is much better because of you.

In loving memory of Tony Trainer.
Sixty years wasn't nearly long enough.

glowing with pleasure. "I knew the minute I saw you, you were the person for this place. I've been praying about it, mind you. So it didn't surprise me when Glenda called and said she might have a renter. Here, I've brought you a welcome gift. Pecan pie and some things to stock your cupboards."

"You didn't have to—"

"Of course I didn't. I *wanted* to. I'll leave everything in the kitchen. Gotta scoot. Prayer meeting in a half hour. Call me if you need something."

"I will. Thank you."

"See you at church Sunday? You did say you planned to attend Grace Christian?"

The nerves that Raven had held at bay for a week clawed at her stomach. "Yes. I'll see you then."

"I knew it. Just knew this would work out." Then Nora was gone as quickly as she'd come, her squat, square figure disappearing around the corner of the house.

In the wake of her departure, the morning silence seemed almost deafening. Humming a tune to block out the emptiness, Raven bent to lift the dirty sheet and caught sight of a strange print in the barren, muddy earth. A footprint—each toe clearly defined, the arch and heel obvious. Small, but not a child's foot. Someone had walked barefoot through the yard, despite the lingering winter chill from the damp spring morning.

Who? Why? Raven searched for another print and found one at the edge of the lawn. From there, a narrow footpath meandered through sparse trees, the prints obvious on earth still wet from last night's rain. She followed the path until it widened and Smith Mountain Lake appeared, vast and blue, the water barely rippling. There, on a rickety dock that jutted toward the center of the lake, was her quarry—white hair, white skin, a bathing suit covering a thin back.

Raven hurried forward. "Are you all right?"

"Thea?" The woman turned, wispy hair settling in a cloud around a face lined with age. "I've been waiting forever. Didn't we agree to meet at ten?"

Ten? It was past noon. Two hours was a long time to sit half clad in a chilly breeze. Raven's concern grew, the nurse in her cataloguing what she saw: pale skin, goose bumps, a slight tremor. "Actually, I'm Raven. I live in the cottage up the hill."

"Not Thea's cottage? She didn't tell me she had guests."

"She probably forgot. Were you planning a swim?"

"Thea and I always swim at this time of year. Though usually it's not quite so cold."

"It *is* chilly today. Here, put this on." Raven slid out of her jacket and placed it around the woman's shoulders.

"Do I know you?"

"No, we haven't met. I'm Raven Stevenson."

"I'm Abigail Montgomery. Abby to my friends."

"It's nice to meet you, Abby. Would you like to join me for tea? I've got a wonderful chamomile up at the house." Raven held out her hand and was relieved when Abby allowed herself to be pulled to her feet.

"Chamomile? It's been years since I had that."

"Then let's go." Raven linked her arm through Abby's and led her toward the footpath, grimacing as she caught sight of her companion's feet. Torn and dirty, they looked painful and swollen. Another walk through the brambles would only make things worse. "It looks like you've forgotten your shoes."

Abby glanced down at her feet, confusion drawing

her brows together. Then she looked at Raven, and behind her eyes past gave way to present. Raven had seen it many times, knew the moment Abby realized what had happened. She waited a beat, watching as the frail, vague woman transformed into someone else, stronger and much more aware.

"I've done it again, haven't I." The words were firm but Abby's eyes betrayed her fear.

"Nothing so bad. Just a walk to the lake."

"Dressed in a bathing suit? In…" Her voice trailed off, confusion marring her face once again.

"It's April. A lovely day, but a bit too cold for a swim."

"What was I thinking?" Frustration and despair laced the words.

"You were thinking about summer. Perhaps a summer long ago."

"Do I know you?"

"My name is Raven. I live up the hill at the Freedman cottage."

"Raven. A blackbird. Common. You're more the exotic type, I'd think, with that wild hair and flowing dress."

Raven laughed in agreement. "I've been fighting my name my entire life. You're the first to notice."

"Am I? Then I guess I'm not as far gone as I'd thought." Despite the brave words, the tears behind Abby's eyes were obvious, the slight trembling of her jaw giving away her emotions.

Raven let her have the moment, watched as she took a deep shuddering breath and glanced down at her bathing suit.

"I suppose it could be worse. At least I wore clothes this time. Now, tell me, where are we headed?"

"To the cottage for tea."

"Let's go, then."

"Here, slip my shoes on first."

"Oh, I couldn't. What about you?"

"I've got tough skin." Raven slid her feet out of open-heeled sneakers and knelt to help Abby put them on. "They're a bit big, but we'll have your own for you in no time at all."

They made their way up the steep incline, Raven's hand steady against Abby's arm. It hurt to know that the woman beside her was being consumed by a disease that would steal her vitality and leave nothing behind but an empty shell. Why? It was a question she asked often in her job as a geriatric nurse. There was no answer. At least none that she could find, no matter how hard she prayed for understanding.

"Sometimes it just doesn't happen the way we want."

"What?" Startled, Raven glanced at Abby.

"Life. It doesn't always work out the way we want it to. Sad, really. Don't you think?"

Yes. Yes, she did think it was sad—her own life a sorry testament to the way things could go wrong. Raven wouldn't say as much. Not to Abby with her stiff spine and desperate eyes. Not to anyone. "It can be, yes. But usually good comes from our struggles."

"And just what good will come of me losing my marbles, I'd like to know?"

"We've met each other. That's one good thing."

"That's true. I've got to admit I'm getting tired of not having another woman around the house."

"Do you live alone?"

"No, I forget things, you know. I live with…I can't seem to remember who's staying with me."

"It's all right. The name will come to you."

Of course, it wasn't all right, was never all right when someone's memory had gaping holes in it. But Abby seemed disinclined to discuss it further. Instead she gestured to the cottage that was coming into view.

"There it is. I haven't been inside in ages. Have you lived here long?"

"I moved in this morning."

"You remind me of the woman who used to live here."

"Do I?"

"Thea. Such a lovely person. It's sad. So sad." The vague look was back in Abby's eyes. Raven saw it as she helped her up the steps to the back door. Was someone out searching for the woman? Raven hoped so, as she had no idea where Abby lived. Nora probably knew. She'd call her after she got her guest settled.

She led Abby through the laundry room and kitchen, into the living room. "Is there anyone I should call? Someone who might be worried?"

Abby didn't respond, just sat on the couch, lost in a world Raven wasn't part of.

"Let's take care of your feet, then I'll make tea." She cleaned and dressed the cuts, then helped Abby lie down. "Rest for a while. I won't be long."

Abby blinked up at her, then smiled. "You're very kind and have a nurse's touch."

"I am a nurse."

But Abby had already closed her eyes and drifted into sleep.

"What do you mean, she's gone? You're being paid to take care of her. Not lose her."

"She was watching TV, just as lucid as could be.

Asked me to run out and get her some chocolate ice cream. I thought she'd be fine for a few minutes."

"Martha." Shane Montgomery stopped, raked a hand through his hair and took a calming breath. "We talked about this when I hired you. Aunt Abby *cannot* be left alone."

"I know. I'm sorry. I'm so sorry." Martha's quiet sniffles turned to deep sobs. "I thought she'd be fine. I never imagined… What if she's gone to the lake? What if she drowns? It'll be on me. On my head. Lord, forgive me."

Shane bit back impatience. He didn't deal well with hysterics and that was where Martha was heading, her round face red and wet with tears. "Let's not panic yet. Aunt Abby has gone off before. She always comes home. There's no reason to believe she won't do the same this time."

Except that Abby had gotten worse in the past months. So much worse that Shane was beginning to wonder if home was the best place for her. Unfortunately there wasn't another option. He'd made a promise to her. He'd keep it. "Let's call the police. Get them started on the search. Then we'll—"

The phone rang, adding fuel to Martha's fear. "What if it's the police? What if she's dead? It'll be my fault. My fault."

"Calm down, Martha. I won't be able to hear above your crying." Shane grabbed the phone on the third ring. "Hello."

"Is this Shane Montgomery?" The voice was soft and pleasant.

"Yes."

"My name is Raven Stevenson. I'm renting the

Freedman property. Nora said you have an aunt. Abigail Montgomery."

"That's right."

"She's here at the cottage with me. I'm afraid she got a bit confused and—"

"I'll be right there."

Shane knew he was being rude, knew he should have given the woman a chance to speak, but his relief at knowing his aunt was safe overwhelmed his social skills. Not that he had many to begin with.

"Is she—?" Martha's voice trembled, her wide brown eyes still overflowing with tears.

"She's all right. I'm going to get her. Do me a favor and brew some of that tea she likes. What's it called?"

"Chamomile?"

"That's the one. I shouldn't be more than a few minutes."

He knew the cottage. Had been there as a child and had no trouble finding it now. The driveway was still dirt and gravel, the house still pale yellow. Shane pulled up close to the porch and hopped out of his Mustang convertible.

The front door opened before he had a chance to take a step, and a woman walked out. *Flower child.* That was Shane's first impression. Curly, untamed hair, flowy confection of a dress, and bare feet scraped and covered with dirt. He figured her to be flighty, naive, maybe a little scattered. Then he met her gaze and was surprised at the calm intelligence he saw there.

"You must be Shane." Her voice still sounded pleasant, though decidedly cooler than it had on the phone.

"And you're Raven."

"Yes. Come in." She stepped aside, allowing him to pass.

He caught a whiff of something flowery and light, heard the rustle of her dress as he brushed by, and thought of summer nights and fancy parties. Then he saw Abby and froze. She looked frail. Old.

"What am I going to do with you, Aunt Abby?"

Raven heard the pain in those words and her judgment shifted. She'd thought the man careless, unconcerned, but realized now she'd been wrong. She moved beside him, placed a hand on his arm and was surprised by a jolt of feeling. She'd thought herself immune to men, hoped herself immune.

Apparently she'd been wrong. She dropped her hand, but couldn't resist the urge to comfort. "She's all right. No harm was done."

"No? I disagree. Look at her. Sleeping like a baby. How will she feel when she wakes up, not knowing where she is? Maybe not even knowing *who* she is?"

She sensed his frustration. He wanted to fix things, couldn't, and was angry at his own inability. Raven could understand that. She was ready to say as much, when Abby surged off the couch, screeching, screaming, arms flailing as she lunged across the room.

"Dead! Thea's dead!"

Chapter Two

Raven sidestepped, not quite avoiding the clawed fingers aimed at her face. Heart hammering, she moved behind the older woman, brushing against Shane who'd leaned in to help, and slipping an arm around Abby's waist. "It's okay, Abby. You're dreaming. Wake up now. Your nephew is here."

As she spoke she led Abby back to the couch and settled her onto the cushions.

"I need to go home."

"Shane's come to take you there."

"Shane? Such a fine boy. It's been years since I've seen him, you know."

"Well, you're in luck today. He's here." Raven wished the man would take his cue and step forward instead of watching with such concentration.

"Really?"

"Yes. Right there."

She gestured in his direction and Shane finally got the hint, hurrying forward and placing a kiss on his aunt's cheek.

"Aunt Abby. I've been worried about you."

"Then you should have come to visit. I've missed you."

"And I you. Come on, let's go home." He held out a hand and helped his aunt up, the look on his face more gentle than Raven would have believed possible from such a big, hard-looking man.

"Let me get some slippers for Abby's feet."

"I'm fine, dear. Don't bother yourself."

"Bare feet again, Aunt Abby? We're going to have to do something about that. Can't have you walking around town with your toes hanging out." Shane smiled down at his aunt, kindly, smoothly taking the decision out of her hands.

Still, it stung. Raven could see it in the sudden coolness of Abby's eyes. Her memory might be going, but pride still lived in the woman's soul.

"I think I have just the thing." Raven grabbed some sandals from the closet and held them out. "Perfect for a sunny day."

"Lovely. Thank you, dear."

Raven helped Abby slide her feet into the shoes, conscious of Shane's gaze. When she straightened, she met his eyes and was surprised by the intensity she saw there. "She's all set."

"Thanks. I'll return the sandals to you this evening."

"Don't worry about it. I won't miss them."

"I'll return them." He put a hand under Abby's elbow and led her outside.

Raven closed the door and released the breath she'd been holding. There was something about Shane Montgomery that threw her off balance, made her jittery and tense. She didn't like the feeling. She didn't like it at all.

A harsh knock sounded at the door. Raven pulled it

open, then stepped back. Silhouetted in the doorway Shane seemed even larger than he had before.

"I forgot to thank you. I do appreciate what you've done. Aunt Abby is…" His voice trailed off.

"She's your aunt. A wonderful, strong, funny woman."

"Yes. She is. It's just harder to see that sometimes. Sorry about your cheek."

His finger skimmed across her stinging flesh. Gentle, tender. Just as his touch had been with Abby.

But Raven was caregiver, not invalid, and she shifted away, uncomfortable with the gesture. "It's nothing."

"It's something and I'm sorry it happened. Now, I'd better get her home."

This time Raven waited at the door until the car disappeared from sight, wondering about the man who drove it. Shane seemed both gruff and caring. Devoted to his aunt, yet already burdened by her care. Would he be the kind to turn his back when the already rocky road got rockier? Would he stick it out until Abby didn't know him anymore? Until she didn't know herself? Or would he be one of the few that stayed until the last breath?

Raven wouldn't even try to guess. Shane and Abby were family, and family was something she had little experience with, something she'd come to Lakeview, Virginia, to learn about. If she dared.

Her hands trembling just a little, she walked to the phone and picked up the phone book that sat beside it. She didn't need to read the circled number. She'd memorized it earlier, had fought with herself about whether to call. Was still fighting with herself.

Had he changed much? As a scared eight-year-old,

she'd seen Ben as a father, not a brother. It wasn't until years later that she'd realized how young he'd been. Perhaps to him, being taken from their home had been a blessing. Perhaps he wanted nothing more than to put that part of his life behind him. If so, did Raven want to know? She'd been disappointed so many times in her life. Each time had hurt just a little more. Now she wondered if it would be better to forget the idea of reconciliation with her brother. Leave things as they had been so many years ago when she was too young to know that knights in shining armor were as tarnished as the rest of the world.

But it was too late to back out. She was here. All she had to do was work up the courage to reach for what she so desperately wanted—family.

Muscles tense with anxiety, she picked up the phone and dialed the number. Then closed her eyes as the phone rang. Once. Twice.

"Grace Christian Church, Penny speaking. May I help you?"

Raven swallowed hard and forced words past the fear in her throat. "Yes, I was wondering if Pastor Ben Avery is in today."

"He is. Would you like to speak with him?"

"No. Well, yes, but I'd prefer to speak to him in person."

"I'm sorry. His schedule is full. Would you like me to take a message?"

"Will you deliver it to him now? It's very important."

"Yes. Of course."

"Tell him Raven called. Tell him I'm on my way to the church."

"I—"

"Thank you." Raven hung up, grabbed a sweater from the closet, slid her feet into clogs and walked out the door.

She didn't think, didn't plan. What good would it do? Life had a way of happening in exactly the way it was meant to. No matter how hard one fought against it.

The church parking lot was nearly empty, the man standing in the center even more noticeable because of it. Faded blue jeans, a dark sweatshirt, sandy hair just a bit long, he watched Raven's car as she parked near the church. Watched as she got out. Even from a distance she could see his eyes—startling blue in a tan, handsome face.

And she knew. Knew before he took the first step, before he sprinted across the area that separated them. Ben. Older, broader. A man now, not a boy, but still it was Ben running toward her, pulling her into his arms. The embrace so familiar, yet completely different.

"Raven." No shout of joy. Just a whisper against her hair.

She pressed her cheek against the thud of Ben's heart, wrapping her arms around his waist, pretending for just a moment that twenty years didn't separate them.

They stood that way for several minutes. Then Ben pulled back, loosening his hold but not letting go. "Do you know how long I've been praying for this?"

His gaze skimmed her face, her hair, the flowing dress she wore. "You're all grown up. And beautiful."

"Not beautiful."

"Yes, beautiful. Come inside. We've got a lot of catching up to do."

And as easily as that, he accepted her.

Raven allowed herself to be led through the church

hall and into an office. A slim blond woman looked up as they walked in, her green eyes narrowing as she caught sight of Ben's arm draped across Raven's shoulder.

"Penny, this is my sister, Raven."

"Sister?" Penny's face relaxed and she stood, her hand extended in greeting. "I had no idea you had a sister, Ben. It's a pleasure to meet you."

"A pleasure to meet you, too."

"Are you in town for a visit?"

"I—"

"No third-degree today, Penny. I'm going to grab my things and head home. Can you call Jim Ross? See if he minds filling in on visitation today."

"Of course."

Ben nodded, then ushered Raven into a small room. "This is my office, such as it is."

She imagined him sitting behind the old wood desk, his brow furrowed in concentration as he worked at the computer. Imagined him standing in front of a congregation, preaching, teaching, ministering. It fit.

Her brother the pastor.

"You're smiling. What are you thinking?" He spoke as he grabbed a briefcase and led her back out of the office.

"That this fits you. The church. The office." They stepped into the hall, and Raven leaned close. "Even the jealous receptionist."

"Jealous? Penny?" He laughed. "She's got bigger fish to fry. Last I heard she was dating a doctor. You still like pink lemonade?"

"It's my favorite."

"You're in luck, then. I always keep a pitcher of it in the fridge. My house is right through those trees."

Decorated in neutral tones, the small, one-level house

didn't seem to reflect anything about the owner. No photos. No knickknacks. Just clean white walls, a few tasteful prints and comfortable furniture.

"Have a seat. I'll be right back."

Raven did as she was asked, easing down onto the sofa and trying hard to look relaxed. Ben was both brother and stranger to her. That made things awkward.

"You're sad." He handed her a tall glass of lemonade and sat beside her.

"A little. You're not the big brother who gave me piggyback rides to the grocery store and bandaged my scraped knees."

"I know. And you're not the little girl with braids and ribbons. But we're still siblings. Still family."

"That's why I came."

"Then there's nothing to be sad about."

"We're strangers, Ben. Not family."

"Families are built. One day at a time. One experience at a time."

"You seem so…accepting about this."

"I guess I'm too happy for anything else. When I got your letters I thought—"

"Letters?" Raven felt the breath catch in her lungs.

"Six or seven years ago. You said you'd contact me if and when you were ready."

"I didn't write you."

"I kept the letters. Come on, I'll show you." He led Raven down a short hall and into a room that was almost a replica of his office at the church. "Take a look."

There were four letters, each dated more than six years ago. Each typewritten with Raven's name scrawled across the bottom.

"I didn't write these."

"Sit down. You're pale as a ghost." Ben pressed her down into a chair and crouched in front of her, his vivid eyes filled with concern. "Tell me. If you didn't write the letters, then who?"

"My husband."

"I'd wondered."

"Did you?" Raven ran a hand through her hair, felt the tangles and wished she'd tied it back prim and proper, the way she'd worn it for so many years. "I didn't. I just assumed what Jonas told me was true. That you'd forgotten all about me. Gone on with your life."

"You married young."

"Not so young. I was twenty."

"And your husband was what? Forty?"

"You seem to know an awful lot about my life."

"Want me to tell you more? Mom regained custody of you the year after we were taken away. You lived in Chicago. Then Baltimore. You graduated high school there, at the top of your class, a year ahead of your peers. Four years later you received a degree in nursing from the University of Maryland. Married the same year. A doctor."

"Like I said, you know a lot about my life."

"I cared, Raven. There's never been a time that you weren't in my heart and mind. It just took me a long time to find you. Mom—"

"Was Mom." Raven didn't want to dredge up the past. Didn't want to open the old wounds.

"She didn't have credit cards. Didn't use her real name most of the time. It was hard to track you down. Once I found you I tried to call. You didn't want to talk to me. At least that's what your husband told me. So I wrote a year's worth of letters. And at the end of that year, I got those—" Ben gestured to the folder Raven held.

She wanted to offer an explanation, to tell him the truth about her life with Jonas, but she wouldn't. Her past was something she didn't share. "I'm sorry Jonas lied to you."

"Don't apologize for your husband. Let him do that."

"He died three years ago."

"Now it's my turn to say I'm sorry. I lost my wife over five years ago. I know how much it hurts."

"Were you married long?"

"Two years. Not nearly long enough." There was sadness in his eyes, but he smiled anyway. "At least I have some wonderful memories. How about you?"

"I have memories."

He eyed her for a moment, his gaze intense. Then, as if sensing her reluctance to discuss her marriage, he stood and held out a hand to pull her to her feet. "You left your lemonade in the other room. Let's go get it."

The phone rang as they walked back into the living room, the answering machine greeting cutting in after the second ring. Then Raven heard, "Hey, Ben. It's Ray. Mom and Dad said you were flying in tomorrow. Said I should pick you up. What time's good?"

Mom? Dad? She ran the words through her mind as Ben reached for the phone.

"Hi, Ray. Listen, my sister's here—Yeah. I can't believe it, either. Can you tell Mom and Dad I can't make it this year? I don't know. Maybe. Listen. I'll call you tonight and tell you more. Bye."

He hung up the phone and smiled at Raven. "Sorry about that. My foster family has a reunion every year. Ray's in charge of coordinating it this time."

"It starts tomorrow?"

"Yes. Two weeks at Camp Remington. Fifty adults. Dozens of kids. Lots of food."

"You're not going to cancel because of me?"

"I'm going to cancel because I want to."

"Ben, no."

"I see my foster parents every few months, the rest of the family a couple of times a year. They won't miss me."

"Please don't cancel. I just arrived, I'm still settling in. I've got unpacking to do. A job to find."

"I can help you with all that."

"I need to do this on my own. Go to your reunion. Enjoy yourself. When you come back, we'll talk more."

He was going to refuse, Raven could see it. A memory flashed through her mind. Ben, much younger, but just as determined, begging the grocer to give Raven a sandwich from the deli. He'd been tenacious. Unwilling to take no for an answer.

The boy lingered in the eyes of the man.

But time must have tempered Ben's will. He nodded. "I can see you need some time. I'll give it to you. But just the two weeks. Then we talk. And I want your phone number, so I can call. Otherwise I'll think this was all a dream."

Raven smiled at his words, some of her tension easing. "You're still bossy."

"And you're still my little sister. Which gives me the right to boss you. Come on. Let's go into town. There's a great diner there. We'll get some lunch and I'll show you around."

He flung his arm around Raven's shoulder, the gesture so right, so natural, that for a moment she could almost believe they'd never been apart.

Chapter Three

By the time Raven returned to the cottage, daylight had given way to evening shadows. She stood on the front porch, her gaze drawn to the horizon, watching as the last rays of light disappeared. Her time with Ben had been easy and comfortable, their reunion much like she'd always hoped it would be. Still she wondered— at the family he was so much a part of, at the wife he'd loved and still missed.

His path through life had been much different from Raven's. Not easier, but perhaps more filled with love. She didn't envy Ben, she only wished she'd made better choices in her own life, and that she were as content and at peace as her brother.

Somewhere in the distance a dog barked, the sound breaking into Raven's thoughts and jarring her mind away from regrets and disappointments. A good thing. Life was too short to waste time worrying about things that couldn't be changed.

It was only later, as she lay wrapped in spring-scented sheets, that the questions she'd shoved to the back of her mind surfaced again. Was Ben really happy to have her in Lakeview? Or was she a bump in the smooth road of his life? His reaction had been open and loving, but still Raven couldn't shake the feeling that she'd intruded on his well-ordered and contented existence. Perhaps leaving Lakeview before Ben returned from his family reunion was the best thing she could do for both of them.

She took a deep, calming breath. She'd spent so much time praying about this, so much time wondering if finding her brother was the right thing to do, she wouldn't second-guess her decision, wouldn't torture herself with the possibilities. Only God knew what the next few months would bring. All Raven could do was wait and see.

With a frustrated sigh, she pushed the sheets off and went into the living room. Her Bible lay on the coffee table and she picked it up, opening to the Psalms and losing herself in words of comfort, in promises of hope, until finally, her eyes closed and she drifted to sleep.

She was there again. In the room at the top of the stairs. Already decorating. Jonas said she was silly and frivolous. That twenty-three weeks was too soon to plan for the new life that grew inside her. She didn't care. She was so happy. Finally, a baby! She'd begged, pleaded for so long to have this chance.

Something creaked outside the door. A loose floorboard that Raven knew meant he was awake. Her heart beat heavily. Would he be angry that she'd left the bed and come here to finger tiny baby booties? The door crashed open and a baby's cry filled the air.

Raven started awake, biting off a scream before it took wing. Sweat beaded her brow and layered her skin,

seeping into the cotton of her nightgown and making it
cling uncomfortably. She needed to get up, to move. To
run from the memories that haunted her dreams. The
high-pitched wail of an infant followed her as she fled
across the room and opened the bathroom door. She'd
take a shower. Cool her skin, ease her tension and block
out the sobs that echoed through the night.

She paused with her hand on the faucet. Sobs. Not
wails. Loud, bitter, hopeless. Definitely not a baby, but
someone... Not a dream, but reality.

Heart in her throat, Raven stepped out of the bathroom and strained to hear the sound again. There it was,
faint but still audible. She hurried to the front door, hes-
itating with her hand on the knob. Was this a trick?
Some bizarre scheme to get her to come outside? She
grabbed the long-handled umbrella from the coat closet,
swung it over her shoulder and pushed the door open.

The sobs were coming from the side of the house.
Raven followed the sound, moving cautiously in the darkness. Bright stars speckled the moonless sky, pinpricks of
light against the blackness. Someone crouched at the far
edge of the house, a dark shadow beside the pale siding.

"Hello? Are you okay?"

No response came. Just the same long, bitter sobs.

"Are you hurt? Lost?"

The person straightened and lurched into Raven with
enough force to knock her backward and onto the
ground. The umbrella flew from her hand and she
twisted, scrambling to find it, her heart thudding pain-
fully, a scream catching in her throat.

"Thea. Thea."

The name was familiar, the trembling voice one
Raven recognized. "Abby?"

The soft cries continued.

"Are you all right? Are you hurt?" Raven spoke as she eased from Abby's grasp, moving gently so as not to hurt her fragile neighbor.

"She's dead. Dead. The blood. What have I done?"

Raven went cold at the words, her hands sliding along Abby's arms, her face, then across the silky material of the blouse she wore. No blood. At least none Raven could feel or see in the dark. Relieved, she grabbed Abby's hand and helped her to her feet. Then put an arm around her waist and led her toward the house. "Let's go inside. Make sure you're not hurt."

"She's dead. She's dead." The mantra continued as they walked into the living room, Abby's quiet chant a chilling background to the too-fast beat of Raven's heart.

"Who's dead, Abby?"

But Abby was gone, her eyes unfocused, reality lost somewhere in the depths of the mind that was failing her. Raven checked her for injuries, found nothing but layers of dirt caked on her hands and streaked across her face. She'd worn shoes this time and they, too, were covered with grime.

"Where have you been, Abby? What have you been doing?" Raven asked the question as she brushed dirt from the woman's cheek. She expected no answer.

"Making amends." The words, whispered on a sigh, hung in the air.

Raven met Abby's gaze. She was there again, in the moment, her dark eyes begging something from Raven.

"What do you need? How can I help you?"

But the moment was already gone, the shift as quick and unstoppable as a wave cresting over the shore. "Where am I? What's happening?"

"You're at the cottage."

"I'm tired."

"Then why don't we get you back home. I'm sure Shane is wondering where you are." At least Raven hoped he was. That Abby had wandered from home twice in less than twenty-four hours didn't say much for the kind of care she was getting.

That bothered Raven. A lot.

She grabbed the phone and dialed the number she'd written down earlier. The phone rang several times before an answering machine picked up. Frustrated, Raven turned to Abby. "Do you live nearby, Abby?"

"Oh, yes. Just down the road a bit. I used to walk here all the time. Thea's mother made the best cookies and never minded if Thea had friends over. She was a great mother. Very warm and sweet. It was so sad when she died."

"Was she young?" Raven walked into the bedroom and pulled on a pair of jeans.

"In her fifties, I think. Thea came home to care for her. It would have been better if she'd stayed away…" Abby's voice faded to silence, and she didn't speak again as Raven led her outside and into the car.

The long country road was unlit by streetlights. Raven drove carefully, searching for another driveway and finding it easily. "Is this it?"

"Yes. Born here. Grew up here. Raised a son here. And I'll die here."

"Not for a long time, I'm sure."

"Life passes quickly. More quickly for some than for others."

Raven glanced in Abby's direction, but in the dark she could see little of the older woman's expression.

A porch light glowed a welcome as Raven pulled up in front of a large house. "Ready?"

"I'm tired, dear. You go on inside."

Raven didn't bother arguing. If Abby felt as tired as she did, the prospect of walking up the porch steps would be daunting. "I'll get Shane."

There was no answer when she rang the doorbell, and she twisted the knob, hoping the door was unlocked. It wasn't. She waited another minute and then went back to the car.

"Abby, do you know where Shane is?"

"Shane?" Abby turned at the name, her eyes wide and filled with pleasure. "Is he in town?"

"Yes. I thought he might be staying with you."

"I don't remember seeing him."

"Do you have a key to the house?"

"A key? I'm sure I do."

"Do you know where it is?" Raven's teeth chattered on the words, the chilly night air seeping through her nightgown. She should have worn a jacket. Would have if she hadn't been in such a hurry to get Abby home.

"I think I do, but I can't remember."

"That's okay, I'm sure we can find a way into the house."

"Good. I'm very tired."

"Let's go around back and see if there's an open door."

"I'll stay here. You go."

Not a bad suggestion, but Raven didn't dare leave Abby alone. "I know you're tired, Abby, but we have to do this together."

"Why? Because I need a babysitter?" A sharp edge was there, almost hiding the fear.

"No, because I don't know the house or the grounds. We can do a much quicker job together."

"I'm too tired. You go."

Raven bit back a sigh and rubbed her hand against the back of her neck. She'd faced this kind of situation before. That didn't make it any easier. She'd ring the doorbell one more time. If that didn't work she'd have no choice but to bring Abby back to the cottage.

As she took a step toward the house she saw a dark figure stroll around the corner.

"What's going on? Who's out here?"

Shane. Finally. "Raven Stevenson. I'm with your aunt."

"What? Why…? Never mind." He came toward them, his movements easy and fluid. "Aunt Abby, you're supposed to be asleep."

"I went for a walk. This kind young lady brought me home."

"Let's get you inside."

Shane leaned past Raven, his shoulder brushing against her arm as he lifted his aunt from the car. "Let's go."

"I don't need to be carried, young man. I'm not an invalid."

"You're a damsel in distress. Let me play gallant knight."

"You always were silver-tongued."

Shane laughed, the sound vibrating through the predawn air. "True." He glanced at Raven as he stepped toward the house. "You coming in?"

She wanted to say no. Wanted to go back to her warm house and her comfortable bed and pretend she didn't care about Abby Montgomery. She couldn't do it. There were things that needed saying. Things that couldn't wait.

"Yes."

Shane didn't go in the front door as Raven had expected, but went back around the side of the house, carrying Abby as if she were featherlight. Raven followed him across the backyard toward a large outbuilding, feeling uncomfortable in a way she hadn't with other patients, in other homes. But then, Abby wasn't a patient.

"My office is above the garage. I do most of my work there. Looks like that might have to change." There was pain, regret and a tinge of frustration in his voice.

Raven had heard them all before, had watched others experience the same during the past three years. But she couldn't allow her empathy to stop her from saying what needed to be said. Abby needed proper care. Without it she'd continue to wander off, and eventually she might not return.

An outside staircase led to the upper level of the garage. Raven followed Shane up and into a large room, her gaze caught and held by myriad prints lining one wall. Colorful, bold, striking. All scenes from some fantasy adventure.

"Scenes from my books."

"What?" Raven turned to Shane.

He'd settled Abby on a long couch and covered her with a blanket, his hand lingering for just a moment on her cheek. "The prints. They're scenes from the books I write."

"You're an author?"

"I write inspirational fantasy adventures for kids." He stepped to the back of the room and gestured Raven over. "Abby's asleep. Let's go in the kitchen."

"I'd rather not leave her alone."

"And I'd rather not have her wake and hear us talking about her. Life is hard enough for her right now."

Shane stepped through the doorway before Raven could argue further.

She hesitated, then followed.

The tiny kitchen sported a sink, a microwave and a small refrigerator. There wasn't room for much more, and barely space for two people to move comfortably. Raven didn't move. Just stood in the doorway, eyeing the man whose presence seemed to fill the kitchen. Jonas had been like that—so vital that everything around him paled in comparison.

"She wasn't alone, you know."

Raven blinked, tried to focus on Shane's words. "Alone?"

"Isn't that what you've been waiting to accuse me of? Leaving my aunt alone. Letting her wander around by herself when she needs to be supervised every moment of the day." His words weren't angry, just tired.

Raven could understand that. In the last days of Jonas's illness she'd been tired, too. But not for the same reasons. "I don't want to accuse you of anything. I just want to make sure you understand what you're dealing with."

"Believe me, I know. Abby's been suffering from dementia for two years, and I've been her primary caregiver for the past three months."

"That's a lot of responsibility for one person, Shane."

"I'm not doing it alone. I've hired people to come in and help out when I can't be here."

"That's good, but not just any caregiver will do. You need trained professionals."

Shane leaned against the counter. "Obviously you're right. She's wandered twice today."

"Does she have other family? Other people who could pull shifts?"

"Abby's son, Mark—but he'd rather have her in an assisted living facility than spend time caring for her. A few months ago he was ready to sell the house and move Abby."

"And you said no?"

"Abby could never stand the thought of moving. I promised that if the time ever came when she couldn't care for herself, I'd take care of her. That time is now. What choice do I have but to follow through with what I said?"

Plenty. Promises were as easily broken as they were made. "I understand you want to care for your aunt, but sometimes home isn't the best place for a person with Abby's problems."

"In this case it is." He straightened, opened the refrigerator and grabbed a soda. "Want one?"

"No, thanks."

"I'm sorry Abby disturbed your rest."

"She didn't. I was already awake."

Shane studied Raven over the rim of the soda can. She looked tired. Dark smudges marred the skin beneath her eyes and her face seemed a shade too pale. The white cotton shift she wore half tucked into a pair of baggy jeans could only be a nightshirt. Obviously she'd tried to sleep. Had worry kept her awake? Nightmares?

That he was curious worried Shane. He had too much to do, too many responsibilities to take on any more. Not that Raven was asking anything from him. On the contrary, she seemed quite capable of taking care of herself and everyone around her.

Did anyone take care of her?

Raven shifted and edged toward the door, nervous, it seemed, in the face of Shane's scrutiny. He set the soda can down, purposely turning away for a moment, giving her the space she seemed to want. "About what happened tonight…"

"You don't have to explain. Even the best caregiver makes mistakes."

"Yeah, well, I'm afraid this time the caregiver in question isn't the best."

"Don't be so hard on yourself, Shane."

He couldn't help it, he laughed, turning to meet Raven's gaze again. "Not me. Not this time, anyway. I hired a college student to stay nights with Abby. Sherri's been reliable and responsible so far. And she says she's a light sleeper and hears Abby when she starts to wander. I'm surprised she didn't this time."

Raven tensed at his words, something that looked like fear in her eyes. "Have you seen Sherri? Talked to her tonight?"

"Earlier. I was getting ready to check on them both when I heard you out front. Why?"

"Abby was hysterical when I found her. Sobbing. Covered with dirt. She said something about a woman being dead. Said it was her fault. It probably means nothing—"

"Stay here. I'll check."

It was nothing. It had to be. There was no way something had happened to Sherri. No way Abby could be responsible for it. Shane ran anyway, down the stairs, across the yard and into the house. The alarm hadn't been set. Setting it was one of the responsibilities of the caregiver and the only way to be sure Abby didn't walk outside at night. Sherri had never forgotten before, so why tonight?

"Sherri?" Shane's heart pounded in his ears as he

waited at the closed bedroom door. He knocked twice and swung the door open.

He wasn't sure what he expected to see. He only knew he was relieved to find Sherri asleep on the fold-out cot.

"You okay?" He nudged her shoulder, his tension easing as she groaned and sat up.

"What? What's going on?"

"I was hoping you could tell *me*." Shane flipped on the light. Saw her flushed cheeks, her bright, glassy eyes. "You feeling okay?"

"I'm all right. Just a scratchy throat." She looked around. Her eyes widened and she leaped from the cot. "Abby. Where is she?"

"A neighbor found her wandering around outside."

"That's not possible. I would have heard the alarm."

"You must have forgotten to turn it on."

"No. I did turn it on."

"Everyone makes mistakes sometimes, Sherri."

"Yeah? Well, not me. Not when it's this important. I turned on the alarm right after you left. My head was pounding and I wanted to lie down once Abby fell asleep, so I punched in the numbers before I even walked out of the foyer."

Shane wouldn't argue the point. There was no sense in it. "Maybe you did. But when I came in a minute ago the alarm wasn't set."

"I don't understand." She shook her head, winced and swayed.

Shane put out a hand to steady her, and was surprised at the heat of her skin. "You're sick. You need to go home. Sit down. I'll get Abby and give you a ride."

"I don't need a ride. Thanks for offering, though."

"Humor me. Stay put until I get back."

He ignored her sputtered protest and headed back outside.

Raven was waiting at the office door, anxiety clear in the fine lines around her mouth and eyes. "Is she all right?"

"She's sick. A fever, headache, sore throat."

"Sounds like strep throat."

"Yeah?"

"That or a viral infection."

"Sounds like you know something about it."

"I'm a home health-care nurse. Or I was. I've taken a leave of absence."

A nurse? Shane didn't know why he was surprised. Thus far, Raven's reaction to Abby had been relaxed, friendly, concerned—all the things Shane would expect from someone used to dealing with patients. But a nurse? It was much easier to imagine her a wandering flower-child.

"I should have guessed that. You've been great with Abby."

"I'll go in and see how Sherri's doing."

"She's in the bedroom at the top of the stairs," he said. "The back door to the house is unlocked."

"I'll check back with you before I leave, just so you know what's going on."

Shane nodded and watched her move across the yard, only turning away after she disappeared inside the house.

Obviously there was more to Raven than flowing dresses and wild curls. But he'd known that when he'd looked into her eyes earlier in the day. What surprised him, what he hadn't expected, was how interested he was in knowing more.

He shook his head. Now wasn't the time for curiosity. Not when he had so many other things occupying his mind. He glanced at the computer, still turned on and begging his attention, eyed his sleeping aunt, looked around at the piles of papers and stacks of mail he needed to sort through.

Raven's suggestion had merit. Professional caregivers could offer round-the-clock assistance for Abby and free up some of Shane's time. But would they *care* about her? And would she be comfortable with people she didn't know? Thus far the caregivers he'd hired were residents of Lakeview, people Abby was familiar with. How would she react to strangers?

"Shane?" Abby's voice trembled from behind him.

He turned toward his aunt, bracing himself for the vagueness he'd see in her expression. Instead she was alert, her gaze bright, curious and maybe just a little scared.

"Hey, you're awake."

"Awake and covered in filth. What happened? Why is all this…?" She gestured to her clothes, the words lost.

"Dirty? You decided to take an early morning stroll."

"Did I?" She spoke on a sigh, her lined face weary. "Well, good for me. Now I think I'll go get in my own…chair."

Shane didn't correct her words, just offered a hand and helped her back to the house and into her room. Raven was still there with Sherri. Both looked up as he entered the bedroom.

"Aunt Abby's ready for bed. I'm going to get her settled."

"Why don't you let me?" Raven spoke as she moved to put an arm around Abby. "Do you mind, Abby? Sherri isn't feeling well."

Her words flowed in soft, comforting waves, and

Shane could imagine her using the same voice, the same tone in her profession.

Abby peered at Raven as if trying to place her face. "I know you, don't I?"

"Yes, I'm Raven."

"A nurse?"

"And a friend. Come on, let's get you cleaned up and settled into bed."

And as quickly as that she took control of the situation.

Sherri mumbled her thanks, refused again Shane's offer to give her a ride home and shuffled from the room.

Shane shifted so she could pass, but remained in the doorway, watching as Raven helped Abby gather clean nightclothes and led her to the adjoining bathroom. He heard the water start. Heard the soft murmur of voices. Saw the weariness on Raven's face when she stepped out of the bathroom.

She left the door ajar and leaned against the door jamb, then straightened when she saw Shane. "I thought you'd gone."

"And leave an obviously exhausted woman to take over my responsibilities? That's not my style."

She shrugged. "I didn't think it was, but I offered to stay with Abby and I'm happy to do it."

"You're not up to it."

"Taking care of people is what I do. Whether I'm up to it or not."

"Not here. Not now. Go home and sleep."

"Abby—"

"Will be fine. I'll stay here until her day companion arrives. Kaylee's an LPN and she's very good with Abby."

Raven shrugged again, the movement emphasizing the thinness of her shoulders beneath the cotton nightshirt she wore. "All right. I'll head out, then. Tell Abby I said goodbye."

"I will." Shane walked her to the door, wondering why he suddenly felt as if he were kicking her out. He'd thought she would be happy to be freed from the responsibility, but instead she seemed reluctant to leave. "Are you okay?"

"I'm fine."

Shane wanted to press for more but knew he had no right. They were strangers, after all. "Thanks again for all you've done for Abby."

"It was no problem." Raven stepped outside and moved toward her car, the shadowy predawn world enveloping her.

Shane caught one more glimpse of her as she opened her car door, the interior light flashing on, her profile illuminated in its glow. She looked worn, lonely and unbearably sad.

He felt a gut-level instinct to go after her, to try to ease the burden that weighed her down. Instead he stood rooted to the spot, unable to turn away. Only when the car disappeared did Shane step back inside the house and close the door.

Chapter Four

The phone rang just after morning light first streaked across the sky. Raven dropped the book she'd been reading and fumbled for the receiver. "Hello?"

"Hey, sis."

"Ben?"

"Yep. Sorry for calling so early. Did I wake you?"

"No. I was reading."

"Still love books, huh?"

"Always. I thought you were leaving this morning?"

"That's why I'm calling. I'll be driving past the Freedman place in five minutes. Mind if I stop in?"

Mind? She'd love it. Anything to fill the empty hours. "You won't miss your plane?"

"Nope. I've got plenty of time. Hold on—I'm here. Took me less time than I thought."

As he said the words, Raven heard the rumble of a motor outside. She rushed to open the door, smiling as Ben got out of a dark blue sedan. "A sedan? I figured you more for a motorcycle."

"I have one of those, too." He came up the stairs and

hugged her hard. "I've been up all night. Afraid if I fell asleep I'd wake up and find out you were just a dream."

"All night?"

"Okay, most of the night. Here—" He passed her a white paper bag. "I brought you something, but you have to share."

"Must be something good."

"It is. Got any coffee?"

"I don't know. I'll check." Raven started toward the kitchen, but Ben stopped her with a hand on her arm.

"Sit down. I'll look."

"Ben—"

"I'm not the only one who's been up all night. Those dark circles under your eyes aren't from a good night's sleep."

"I'm fine."

"And I'm your big brother, which gives me the right to boss you around. We agreed on that yesterday, remember? So sit."

"Suit yourself. I'll just eat everything you brought before you get back."

"Now that would be cruel and unusual punishment. I couldn't allow it and still feel good about myself." He snagged the bag from her hand, pulled out a chocolate-frosted doughnut and handed the bag back. "Everything else is yours. Be back in a minute."

He was back in five. "No coffee, but I did find orange juice. Here."

"Thanks."

"Now, tell me what kept you up all night."

"Do you know Abigail Montgomery?"

"Sure do. She's been in Lakeview longer than either of us has been alive. She used to be active in the community but has had to step back from her responsibilities these past few years."

"Do you know why?"

"I do, but I'm not sure if it's common knowledge and I don't want to break a confidence."

Raven stood and paced the floor. "Then you know she suffers from dementia. That it's gotten worse in the past few months."

"Yes. Shane and I have talked about her condition several times. He's concerned. And rightfully so."

"He definitely should be concerned. Last night Abby wandered from the house. Ended up here, digging around near the side of the cottage, sobbing and crying. I found her and brought her home."

"Thank God."

"That wasn't the first time. I found her on an old dock down by the lake yesterday afternoon. Again, she'd wandered away."

"I thought Shane hired people to help him care for Abby."

"He did. I'm not sure how qualified they are though. At this point, Abby needs professionals. People who understand her condition and are trained to deal with the symptoms."

"Like you."

Raven sat back down on the couch. "It doesn't have to be a nurse. Though that wouldn't hurt."

"Did you tell Shane this?"

"I told him Abby needs more than what she's getting right now."

"He'll hire more qualified people. Shane's that way. He loves his aunt. Wants what's best for her."

"I sense that."

"So Abby's wandering woke you up and you couldn't get back to sleep?"

"There were other things on my mind, but I'm fine now."

"Then maybe you'll consider coming with me today."

"I can't, Ben. I have to get settled. Look for a job. Do a million other little things that come with a move."

It was Ben's turn to pace the room, his movements abrupt, his long legs covering the floor in three long strides. "You were upset yesterday. You can say I'm wrong a thousand times and it won't change what I know."

"No—"

"It isn't because I'm going to the reunion. I know that. So what is it, Rae?"

Rae. Ben was the only one who'd ever shortened her name. She'd forgotten until now, the memories too bittersweet to dwell on. "I felt awkward yesterday. I should have called, set up a meeting, then you wouldn't feel torn between me and your family."

Ben came to a halt in front of her, his blue eyes blazing, the muscle in his jaw tense. "*You* are my family."

"Ben, you call them Mom and Dad. How can they be anything less than family to you?"

The anger seeped out of him as quickly as it had arrived. "So that's what this is all about."

Raven felt petty and jealous. She didn't like the feeling, and her own anger rose because of it. "Yes. *That's* what it's all about."

Ben eyed her for a moment, then took a seat on the sofa. "You remember Vacation Bible School? The year Social Services was called in?"

"Yes." How could she forget? She'd told a kind VBS

worker that Ben took care of her. That her mother was never home. That sometimes there was no food to eat.

"Remember when we prayed? When we committed our lives to Christ? You were young. Only eight."

But old enough to know what it meant. Old enough to understand that even if her mother didn't love and care for her, her Heavenly Father did. That had meant a lot to her as an eight-year-old. "I remember."

Ben nodded, smiled. "I've wondered. Anyway, I was angry when we were separated. Angry with Mom, with the system, even with God. I got into trouble. Spent five years being shipped from foster home to foster home. Spent some time in a group facility. Right before I turned seventeen, Mike Spencer came to see me. Said he and his wife had heard about me and they wanted to offer me a home for as long as I wanted to stay."

"Your foster father?"

"Yeah. I figured anything was better than where I was, so I packed my things and went home with him. I made their lives incredibly hard for a few months, but no matter what I did, no matter how foulmouthed and awful I was, Mike and Andrea never turned away from me."

"It sounds like they're good people."

"Better than good. They're amazing, loving and tough. I might have pushed the limits, but it felt good to know there were some."

"I'm glad, Ben. Glad you found a family, people who love you." And she was, despite her own wish that she'd been there with him. Maybe if she'd had limits and love she wouldn't have made so many mistakes.

"I am, too. But that doesn't mean I don't need you in my life. You're the best of what I remember from childhood. Remembering you, imagining finding you again—that's what kept me from getting involved in the kind of crime that would have put me in jail."

"Good. I'd hate to be visiting you in prison."

"There's that. So, why don't you come with me? Mike and Andrea would be thrilled to meet you. And I'd love to spend more time getting to know you."

"Not this time. I really do have to get settled in and look for a job. But tell them I'm looking forward to meeting them. And thank them for doing such a good job with you."

"I will. And now I'd better get going." He stood and walked to the door, then turned back to Raven as he stepped outside. "If I didn't think you needed space, if I wasn't sure I'd smother you with attention and drive you away from Lakeview before you had a chance to settle in, I wouldn't go. I'd camp out in this house and ask you the million questions that are buzzing through my mind. But you'd run—leave here for someplace where you could think. So I'm giving you the time, Rae. And I'm praying for you."

He was gone before his words could register, before Raven could realize how right he was, and wonder how it was possible he could know her so well after so many years apart.

She waved as he drove away, refusing to acknowledge the sadness she knew she shouldn't feel. She'd found her brother, reunited with him after years apart; her heart should be overflowing with joy. Instead she felt hollow.

It was a feeling she was all too familiar with. Luckily she had a cure—running. It was something she'd been doing both literally and figuratively for years. She could see no reason to change the pattern now. Especially not with the sun bright overhead and a cool spring breeze wafting across the yard.

Ten minutes later she began a slow jog up her driveway and onto the road, increasing her pace as she followed the curves and bends of the country lane. Birds chirped and called to one another, the sounds mixing with the pounding of her feet and the soft gasp of her breath. She lost herself in the rhythm of the run, racing across the pavement until there was nothing in her mind but the pulsing of blood. Then, when she couldn't run another step, she turned and began walking home.

She hadn't gone far when a police cruiser passed and stopped several yards ahead of her. An officer stepped out. "You all right, ma'am?"

"I'm fine. Just out for a stroll."

"Not much around here but trees and grass. You must have walked quite a ways."

He spoke as Raven approached, and she could see the suspicion in his dark blue eyes.

She stopped a few feet from the cruiser, trying hard not to look guilty of something. "I'm renting the Freedman property. It—"

"I know where it is. Like I said, you've walked a long way."

"Not so far. I run marathons. Five or six miles isn't much."

He studied her for a moment longer, as if trying to ascertain the truth of what she was saying. Then he nodded, extending a hand. "I'm Jake Reed. County Sheriff."

"Raven Stevenson."

His eyes flashed recognition, then surprise. "Ben Avery's sister?"

"That's right."

"He know you're in town?"

"Yes."

"Good. You need a lift home?"

The conversational tangents were making Raven's head spin. Or maybe it was fatigue and too much emotion. "No. I'm fine. It's a nice day for a walk."

"It is. But remember, even out here in the country bad things happen."

"It can't be any more dangerous than other places I've lived."

"You're probably right, but it's always best to err on the side of caution."

"And walking along a country road isn't being cautious?"

Sheriff Reed gestured toward an open field to the left of the road. "See that field? Thirty-five years ago a woman went to pick wildflowers on the far hill. She never returned."

"She was murdered?"

"No one knows. Could be she ran away. Could be she was abducted. Could be she was killed. All anyone knows for sure is that she was here one day—the next she was gone."

"Isn't that old news?"

"Stories like that one get told over and over, the plots twisted and changed until the facts are layered with so much embellishment it's hard to tell where one begins and the other ends."

"You must have an opinion about what happened or you wouldn't be warning me to be careful."

"Actually, I would. I'm the cautious type—just ask my wife." He smiled, his face softening.

"I am, too, Sheriff. So don't worry, I'll be careful."

"Call me Jake. Everyone else does. And make sure you're as careful as you say you'll be. Ben would never forgive me if I let something happen to you."

"You and Ben are friends?"

"Friends and fishing buddies."

"I wouldn't want to ruin that."

"Me, neither." He smiled again. "I'd better get back to work. Nice meeting you."

"You, too." Raven took a step away, then turned back. "Jake?"

He stopped, half in, half out of the cruiser. "Yeah?"

"Who was the woman? The one that disappeared, I mean."

"Theadora Trebain. Use to live in the cottage you're renting."

A sudden chill raced up Raven's spine, and the fine hair on her arms stood on end. She didn't realize she'd swayed until Jake strode toward her and put a steadying hand on her arm.

"You okay? You've gone pale."

Raven straightened, stepped away from his touch. "I'm fine. I just wondered if the woman was related to my landlady, Nora Freedman."

"Nora's husband was Thea's cousin. He took care of the property after she disappeared. Guess he always hoped she'd come home."

"Her disappearance must have been hard on the family."

"It was. Though if you ask Nora she'll say the one saving grace was that Thea's mother passed away before it happened."

"It's still a sad story. Whether or not the mother was around to know what happened to her daughter."

Jake didn't respond, just watched Raven, his gaze sharp and focused. Could he hear her heart pounding in her chest? Did he sense that she was withholding information? Should she tell him about Abby's strange ramblings?

The shrill ring of a phone saved her from making a decision. He shifted and grabbed a cell phone from the cruiser. "Reed here."

He listened and smiled, the expression on his face changing so dramatically that he looked like a different person.

"Sure, babe. No. I'll be home in a couple of hours."

His gaze shifted to Raven. "No, no crime. I did meet Ben's sister…me, too. I'll tell her."

He threw the phone back onto the seat. "My wife. She said to tell you hi. Says she hopes to meet you soon."

"Oh, I—"

"Better get used to it. It's the way of things around here. Everyone knows everyone."

Raven nodded. "I got that impression from Nora."

"Nora Freedman's a great lady. And now, I really do have to go. Take care."

Raven watched the cruiser disappear around a curve in the road and only then did she do what she'd been wanting to do all along. She turned toward the field and waded through knee-high grass. The far slope was just beginning to bloom with tiny purple flowers and tall, fluffy dandelions sparse but evident among the green. Raven could imagine what it would be like in a few weeks, the profusion of colors and textures beautiful and tempting.

Had the woman who disappeared seen it this way? Had she wanted to breathe in the soft scent of flowers and earth, and collect some of the beauty that dotted the hillside?

Theadora. Like Raven's own name, Thea's wasn't that common. Raven shivered, her gaze traveling the width and breadth of the field. Questions filled her mind, then scattered as she hiked across the lush landscape, cresting the far hill and slowing as a white farmhouse came into view. A wide porch stretched across the front of the house, and two rocking chairs sat empty on either side of a small table.

"Good morning!" A tall, auburn-haired woman called the greeting as she rounded the corner of the house. "You must be our new neighbor."

"Yes, I'm Raven Stevenson."

"Tori Riley. I heard you'd moved in. What was it? Yesterday?"

"Yes."

"How about some coffee?"

"I—"

"Juice, then? I'm sure you're busy, but Pops will have my head if I don't invite you in."

Before Raven could ask who Pops was, Tori strode to the front door, shoved it open and called inside. "Hey, Pops, we've got company."

"So don't just stand out on the porch, come in."

The voice was gruff and Raven wasn't sure she wanted to meet its owner. "I really don't want to disturb your morning."

"You're not. Pops always sounds like that."

Tori led the way into a bright, airy kitchen. A man stood by the stove, his face lined with age, his eyes deep brown and curious. "This the new neighbor?"

"Yep. Raven Stevenson, meet Sam Riley. Otherwise known as Pops."

"Nice to meet you, Mr. Riley."

"Sam to my friends."

"Sam, then."

"Sit down. I've got coffee or juice. Pancakes, too, if you're hungry."

"Juice would be nice, thanks."

He nodded and poured a glass of orange juice, then slid it onto the table in front of her. "Looks like you were out for a run."

"Yes, it's a beautiful morning for it and the scenery's great."

"Still gotta be careful running by yourself."

"Jake Reed was just telling me that."

"Guess he told you about Thea Trebain."

"Pops, don't start." Tori slid into a chair beside Raven, a plate filled with pancakes in her hand.

"I'm not starting anything. Just warning her to be careful."

"You're getting ready to spin one of your tales."

"It isn't a tale. It's God's truth."

"Your truth, you mean." She turned to Raven. "Don't believe a word my grandfather says about Thea Trebain. He likes to make it sound more mysterious than it is. Most people think she got fed up with small-town life and left."

"Without telling her family? Without packing her bags?"

"None of that is fact, Pops, and you know it."

Their argument seemed an old one, well worn. Their affection for each other peeked through the words, even as their so-alike brown eyes shot flames. The similarity between the two was obvious, the connection between them filling Raven with longing.

She pushed away from the table and stood. "I hate to drink my juice and run, but I'd really better get home."

"Now look what you've done, Tori. You've chased her off."

"Me? You're the one trying to scare her."

"Warn—not scare."

Raven smiled at the banter, forcing aside her own feelings of loneliness. "Neither of you chased me off. It's just time for me to go."

"Now, don't go rushing off, Raven. I've got something for you. A welcome gift. Something a woman who likes to run shouldn't be without. Come on out to the barn, I'll get it for you."

Raven opened her mouth to protest, but Tori shook her head. "You may as well go with him. If you don't, he'll be pounding on your door this afternoon. I've got to run. Work won't wait. Much as I'd like it to sometimes. Maybe we can have lunch."

"I'd like that."

"Great. I'm in the book." She paused, glanced at Sam who was stepping out into the hall. Then she whispered, "And listen, if Pops gives you a gun or a sword, just take it and smile. He means well. I'll get it from you when we have lunch. Gotta run. Bye, Pops." She rushed forward, kissed her grandfather on the cheek, and was gone.

"Come on, Raven. I may be retired but that doesn't mean I've got all day. You're gonna like this. I guarantee it."

Raven quickened her pace and prayed that his granddaughter's prediction about the gift proved false. Guns? Swords? Maybe Jake was right, maybe walking along a country road *wasn't* the safest thing she could have done with her morning.

Chapter Five

A barn stood open behind the farmhouse, a green tractor its only visible occupant. Sam stepped into the dimly lit interior and gestured for Raven to follow.

"This barn used to be filled with farm equipment. Now it's empty. Seems a shame really. Tori plans to till the land again. An organic farm, she says. Should be interesting."

"Your granddaughter seems very nice."

"Nice? Tori? Sometimes. Mostly she's busy. Too busy, if you ask me. She's got a vet business down the road a ways. Works hard."

"She's a vet?"

"One of the best." Sam spoke as he led Raven deeper into the barn. "Up these stairs here. In the loft."

Raven followed, cringing a little as something scurried in a dark corner.

"Now, you've gotta be quiet. Don't want to startle her."

Her? Raven didn't like the way this was going. Didn't like it at all. "Sam—"

"Shh! Come on. Quietly."

What choice did she have? Raven moved up the stairs

behind Sam, wondering how she could gracefully refuse his gift.

"Ah, there she is. Now take a look. And tell me if that isn't just the cutest thing you've ever seen."

He stepped to the side, allowing Raven into the large area and gesturing to a box in the middle of the floor. Something was in it. Something with eyes and fur. Something very, very ugly. Raven took a step back.

"What is it?"

"*It?* It! Gal, use the eyes God gave you. Haven't you seen a dog before?"

"A dog?" It didn't look like any dog Raven had ever seen.

"Of course a dog. What'd you think she was? Come on close and take a look. She's a darling, all right."

Raven inched closer and peered into the box. The animal looked more like a giant rat. Pointy snout, pointy ears and a skinny little tail. "What kind is it?"

"Not it. Her name is Merry. Short for Miracle. Found her on the side of the road tied in a plastic bag. She'd managed to paw through the plastic and had her nose sticking out. Her litter mates weren't so lucky."

"That's terrible."

"Yep. It is. I called the sheriff, but there's nothing he can do. No way to find the person responsible."

"It's kind of you to give her a home."

"Now, see, that's the problem."

Raven braced herself for what was coming. Told herself there was nothing wrong with saying no. Reminded herself that she didn't need or want a dog—especially not one that looked like a rat.

"See, my granddaughter, she's not real happy with all the strays I've been picking up lately. Says I'm run-

ning out of room. She's got a point. I've got three dogs
already. And two cats. I've been bringing strays to her,
and she's done a good job of finding them homes."

"Wonderful. I'm sure she won't have trouble finding
Merry a home. Lots of people are looking for puppies."

"True. True. But Tori made me promise not to bring
any more strays to her office. Told me if I picked up another one I'd have to find it a home myself."

"I bet you've got lots of friends who'd love to have
a dog." Raven backed toward the steps, ready to run
while she had the chance.

"You'd think, wouldn't you? I've had a few over to
take a look at the pup, but they don't see her potential.
I've had her for two weeks and not one person's willing to take her."

Raven could understand why. She took another step
back. "That's too bad."

"I thought so. Then you walked into the kitchen
wearing your running gear and I knew why no one else
wanted Merry."

"You did?"

"Yep. That little gal is meant for you."

"Sam, I—"

"Just take a look and then tell me I'm wrong." He
lifted the puppy, set her on the floor. "See those long
legs? The lean torso? The tail?"

"Uh…yes."

"She's got greyhound blood. Not purebred, but that
makes it even better. She's got the lines, the speed, but
not a timid nature."

"I don't see how—"

"Of course you do. You're a runner. She's a runner.
It's a perfect match."

"But Sam, I've never owned a dog. I wouldn't know what to do with her."

"What's to do? You feed her. Run with her. Give her some love. She'll be your friend for life. Here, just hold her for a minute. *Then* tell me you don't want her."

Raven gritted her teeth and put out her hands to take the puppy, telling herself it was only for a minute—that she'd hold the dog just long enough to find an excuse to say no.

Twenty minutes later she was back on the road, heading home. Merry, sporting a rhinestone collar and faux leather leash, tumbled along behind, her long legs and big feet tangling until Raven gave up and lifted the awkward puppy.

"Greyhound, my eye. You're no more greyhound than I'm a world-class sprinter. That man's a menace. He could sell sand in the desert."

And Raven would probably be the first in line to buy it.

She shifted the dog in her arms and tried not to notice the comfortable warmth against her chest. "I'd rather have a gun or sword. At least that I could hand over to Tori."

The dog wiggled in Raven's hold and turned just enough to lick her cheek. "Oh. Yuck. Hold off on the kisses, mutt. I'm only keeping you as long as it takes to find you a home."

A sporty black car sped around a curve in the road and screeched to a stop a few feet away. The door flew open and Tori Riley jumped out.

"I knew it. I knew that man was up to no good. Got to the office and it all clicked. The secrecy, the sly questions about puppy care. That's one ugly mutt."

"She's not that bad."

"How'd he talk you into taking her?"

"I don't know. One minute I was saying 'no thanks' and the next I was walking home with a puppy."

"Didn't even have the guts to give you a ride home. That's low."

"He was probably afraid I'd come to my senses." Raven glanced down at the wiggling puppy. Merry wasn't *that* ugly. Actually, she was kind of cute…in a homely sort of way.

"Uh-oh. I know that look. You're hooked."

"I'm not. I'm going to find her a home."

"Right. Come on. I'll give you a ride and then take a look at her. Make sure she's healthy. You'll have to make an appointment to have her shots done. The sooner the better."

"Okay. But I'm not keeping her."

"Of course you're not."

Raven shot a look in Tori's direction, but decided not to argue further. The fact was, she was already starting to like the idea of having a dog. She pushed Merry into the car and climbed in behind her. Tomorrow would be soon enough to make a final decision. For now she'd accept the ride that was offered, and be thankful for it.

Shane stepped out of his office, trying hard to control his irritation. He had work to do, plenty of it, before his manuscript could be sent out. The last thing he wanted was a visit from his cousin. Not that he minded Mark stopping by to see his mother. On the contrary, he wished he'd come by more often. Unfortunately, this time he hadn't come alone, he'd brought Adam.

The son of Abby's only brother, Adam was a savvy

businessman and aspiring politician who hadn't had time for his aunt until recently. Now, with election year looming, he made bimonthly visits and mentioned those visits to anyone willing to listen. That bothered Shane. What bothered him more was that Adam had plenty of opinions about Abby's care, but not a lot of ideas about how to help.

He sighed and stepped into the house, following the sound of voices into the parlor. "Hi, Aunt Abby. Mark. Adam."

Abby's smile was vague, her eyes fixed on the television.

Adam didn't bother smiling at all. "She was sitting in front of the television when we got here and she won't budge. Didn't the doctor say she shouldn't spend so much time doing nothing?"

Shane bit back an angry response. "She's enjoying herself. That's what's important."

"Would you let a child sit in front of the television for hours on end?"

"Abby isn't a child."

"That's not the point."

"Then what is? She's almost seventy-three. Shouldn't she be allowed to do as she pleases?"

"Let's not argue. Not in front of Mom. Why don't we let her finish watching the show, and we'll go into the kitchen?" Mark, as always, was the voice of reason.

"Good plan." Adam stalked from the room.

Shane would have followed, but Mark placed a hand on his arm to hold him in place. "He's in a mood today. Says he thinks Mom should be in a facility designed to meet her needs."

"That's not his decision to make."

"Maybe not, but Adam is her nephew. He has a right to voice his opinion."

"I'm her nephew, too. Just because Meade blood doesn't run through my veins doesn't mean I don't want the best for Abby."

"I know. If I didn't believe that, I would have put her in an assisted living facility months ago. I just want you to understand how Adam feels."

"I don't. I can't. Love isn't something you give when it's convenient—"

"Are you two coming? I've got a meeting in half an hour." Adam's voice drifted from the kitchen, cutting off the conversation.

"Just play it cool. You two have never gotten along and I'm not in the mood for an argument," Mark hissed as they walked into the kitchen.

Shane nodded agreement, stepping aside so the caregiver he'd hired for the afternoon could go back into the parlor with Abby.

"We've got a problem." Adam didn't bother with niceties.

"What's that?"

"Abby. Obviously she needs more help than you can give her."

"Obviously?"

"She wandered away again last night, right?"

Shane shrugged, not bothering to ask how Adam had gotten the information. No doubt Sherri had told a friend, who'd told someone else. News traveled fast in Lakeview.

"Adam and I are concerned, Shane. Mom could get lost or hurt."

"I've got an alarm system. I'm not sure what else we can do."

"We can put Abby in Winter Haven." Adam pulled a brochure from his pocket. "I visited there last week. It's—"

"No."

"Hear me out. Winter Haven has qualified, twenty-four-hour staffing—people who know how to deal with someone like Aunt Abby."

"I said no. Abby wants to be home. That's where she should be."

"Come on, Shane, do you think she really cares at this point?" Adam ran a hand through his hair, then carefully smoothed the thick, salt-and-pepper strands back into place.

"Yes. I do. And even if I didn't, I wouldn't shove her away somewhere and let strangers care for her."

"Sometimes it's necessary." Mark sank into a chair and rubbed at the back of his neck. He looked tired, older than his forty years.

Shane sat down across from him. "I know that, Mark. Sometimes it *is* necessary. Sometimes there isn't someone available to be home round-the-clock. Sometimes it gets to be too much of a strain on finances and family. But in this case, none of those things is true."

"Mark's point is, Abby may not always be able to be home. Why not move her now, get her a nice room, let her settle in?"

"Actually, I think that's *your* point."

"Enough." Mark stood, paced the room. "Look, I want the best for Mom. Whatever that might be."

"We all do, Mark." Adam placed a hand on his shoulder, his features schooled into an expression of empathy and concern. "That's why I think—"

"I'll contact the home health-care agency Dr. Mc-

Math recommended and set up twenty-four-hour care for Abby." Shane had given the idea plenty of thought during the night. He might not like the idea of strangers caring for Abby, but it was better than the alternative.

Mark nodded. "I think that's best. Then she can be here and we can be sure she's got proper care, even when you're writing."

"I think you're making a mistake, Mark."

"It's the best decision I can make for now. We'll see how things work out—"

"Oh, I didn't know you were here." Abby spoke from the doorway, a smile creasing her face, her caregiver hovering a few steps behind. "You're just in time for ice cream."

"Sounds great, Mom." Mark led her to a chair, and Shane could see the love he had for his mother. Too bad that love didn't translate itself into time and attention. There was a rift between the two, one Shane didn't understand.

"So you're finally done with the television and now it's ice cream?" Adam kissed Abby on the cheek, his affection seeming less genuine than Mark's.

"You know I love ice cream, Daniel. It's my favorite."

"I'm not Daniel. I'm Adam."

"You shouldn't have done it. We would have worked things out." She grabbed his hand and he yanked it back, stepping away from her.

"Here." He reached into his pocket and pulled out a box. "I brought you something."

"How nice." But she didn't move to open the box.

Shane leaned in. "Need some help with that, Aunt Abby?"

"Lovely."

He pulled the lid off the box and took out a silver necklace. "This'll look great on you."

"Yes. Remember the one Grandmother Meade had? It was very pretty. You gave it to Thea, didn't you, Daniel?"

"I'm not Daniel." He bit out the words and turned to the door. "I have to go."

"I think she's dead…unless it was a dream. I do have vivid dreams, you know."

"Who's dead, Mom?" Mark scooped ice cream into a bowl and slid it in front of Abby.

"She's rambling again. I'm leaving. Goodbye, Aunt Abby."

"Goodbye, Daniel."

Adam stiffened at the name. "It's *Adam,* Aunt Abby. Not Daniel. I need to go."

Shane followed. "She can't help it. Sometimes she's living in the moment. Sometimes in the past."

"That doesn't make it any easier to be called by my father's name."

"From what I've heard, your father was a good man."

"Good? Try coward."

"He was sick. Not a coward. Depression—"

"He wasn't depressed a day in his life. He made a mistake and didn't want to face the consequences of it."

"From what I heard—"

"Right. What you *heard.* You weren't born yet. Have no idea what it was like. I was eighteen. Getting ready to go off to college. Excited about starting an independent life. Then my father kills himself and I'm suddenly the man of the family. If Mom hadn't remarried, I'd still be living at home, taking care of things for her. Look, I don't have time for this right now. I can't be late. See ya." And he was gone.

Which was good, as Shane had had about all he could take of the man.

The old grandfather clock chimed four as he headed back to the kitchen. He needed to get some writing done, but his day help was leaving and the night shift didn't start until six. Maybe Mark could lend a hand.

Shane didn't get a chance to ask. His cousin was already stepping into the hall. "I've got to get home. Laura asked me to pick something up for dinner."

Shane held back the protest that threatened to spill out. "All right."

"Let me know if you need any help with finances. I know full-time caregivers are expensive."

"I'd rather have your time than your money."

"We've been through this before, Shane. Mom doesn't want me here. Doesn't need me here. She's always been more of a mother to you than to me."

It was true and Shane didn't deny it. "I just hope you don't regret it one day."

"Me, too. Call me and let me know what you line up for home health-care." And then he was gone, as well.

"I'm leaving, Shane." Sheila stepped into the hall and looked at the closed door. "Did Mark leave already?"

"I'm afraid so."

"I can stay another hour if it'll help."

"No way. You said you had plans for this evening."

"They can be changed."

"It's your anniversary, right?"

"Dave won't mind."

"Sure he will, but he loves you too much to say so. Go home. I'm fine with Abby."

She hesitated. "As long as you're sure…"

"I am."

"All right. Call me if you need someone to fill in again. You know I've always cared about Abby."

"I know and I appreciate it. Now, go home and enjoy your anniversary."

Abby was seated at the kitchen table when Shane walked back into the room, her gaze vague, the ice cream she'd wanted so much melting into a puddle at the bottom of the bowl. Shane put a hand on her shoulder, wishing he could give her more than time and patience.

"Come on, Aunt Abby. Let's go for a walk. It's a nice evening."

"Yes, I'd like to visit Daniel."

Shane let his hand drop away and leaned down closer to his aunt, not sure where her mind had taken her and how much she remembered about her brother. "Daniel doesn't live around here anymore."

"I want to go to Cemetery Hill."

"In that case, let me get you a sweater."

They took the shortcut down to the lake and walked along the shoreline until they reached the steep slope that led to the Meade family graveyard. It had been years since Shane had taken the path up the hill. Brush and trees had reclaimed most of the once-cleared footpath and the way looked treacherous.

"I don't know, Aunt Abby. The way isn't clear and it might be difficult to get to the graveyard."

"You stay here, dear. I wouldn't want you to get hurt."

"It's not me I'm worried about."

"You worry too much. Let's go."

He might have argued, but something darted from between two trees, a small dark blur that raced toward them. Shane tugged Abby to the side, trying to get her out of the path of the animal, but it seemed intent on reaching them, its pointy nose and overlarge ears quivering with excitement as it skidded across leaf-strewn grass and toppled into a heap at his feet.

A crash of twigs and underbrush warned Shane that something was following. Something big.

Chapter Six

Shane stepped in front of Abby, shielding her from a threat he couldn't yet see. Then he grinned as Raven raced through the trees, her hair flying in a cloud of ebony curls, a long dress billowing around her ankles.

Fear, then recognition flashed across her face as she saw Shane and tried to stop. Her shoes slid on earth and grass, her arms windmilling. Shane put a steadying hand on her waist and tightened his grip. He knew he should release his hold, step back and let Raven have the space she always seemed to need. Instead he moved in, his arm wrapping around her back, holding her still as he stared down into her face. She looked as surprised as he felt. Surprised and just a little afraid.

"It's okay." Shane spoke into the tension, easing away from Raven.

"I'm sorry. My dog…" She glanced over and shook her head. "Merry, don't you dare!"

But the animal was already moving, running and tumbling to Abby, who bent and held out her hand.

"Hello. Aren't you an interesting-looking thing. What is she, Thea, a pharaoh hound?"

"I'm not sure. Just a mutt of some sort."

Raven walked toward the older woman, and Shane was sure she was relieved to be away from him. She knelt beside the puppy, heedless of dirt and grass, and clipped a leash to Merry's collar, then ran a hand along the puppy's short fur.

Strong hands, Shane noted. Small boned, long fingered, but not fragile looking. Not like the rest of her. Shane had felt each vertebra when he touched Raven's back, each rib when his hand grazed her side. She seemed small and insubstantial, incapable of lifting, moving and supporting patients. Yet Shane had seen Raven with Abby and knew she was capable of all those things and more. She was able to care. He'd seen it in her eyes, in the gentleness of her touch.

Would she be willing to help with Abby?

The thought gave him pause and he watched a bit longer as the two women bent over the puppy. For some reason Abby had bonded with Raven in a way she hadn't bonded with any of the local help Shane had hired. That's what Shane wanted for his aunt—a person she liked, that she trusted and felt comfortable with.

He moved toward the two women, ignoring Raven's obvious tension as he bent to scratch the puppy behind its ears. "So this is a puppy."

"What did you think she was?"

"When she came crashing out of the woods I thought she was a big rat."

"She doesn't look anything like a rat." She glared at him, but there was humor in her eyes, and Shane smiled.

"Of course not."

"Sam says she has potential and will be the perfect running companion when she gets bigger."

"Sam Riley?"

"Yes, we met this morning."

"And tonight you're the proud owner of a very interesting-looking dog. Why doesn't that surprise me?"

"Merry's cute, not interesting."

"Doesn't every mother think her baby is the cutest?"

Shane had meant the question as a joke, but Raven stiffened and turned away.

"I need to get back. I hadn't meant to come this far, but Merry took off before I could put her leash on."

"Must you go, Thea? We've barely had time to visit," Abby said.

"Abby, I—"

But Shane didn't let her finish the excuse. He leaned in close, whispering against her ear. "Don't run away yet. Abby's been lonely for someone to talk to."

"She has you."

"I'm a man. It's not the same."

She shrugged, moved a step away. "Where are you heading, Abby?"

"To see the graves."

"Graves?"

Raven looked at Shane and he was struck by the sadness in her eyes.

He nodded. "The Meade family graveyard is at the top of this hill. It's a little steep, though, Abby. Maybe another day would be better."

"No, now is best. Otherwise I might forget."

"I can help." Raven linked an arm through Abby's. "Is this the Meades' land?"

Abby didn't respond and Shane answered for her.

"Abby's land. She's a Meade. Or was until she married my uncle. This piece of land, around two hundred acres, was deeded to her when she married. Her brother owned the land west of here. Now it belongs to Abby's nephew, Adam." Shane spoke as he stepped forward supporting Abby from the other side as they maneuvered up the steep incline.

The information was interesting, but not quite as interesting as the man who'd offered it. Raven glanced in Shane's direction, noting the rough, craggy face and stern expression. Even his voice had a hard edge. Yet his gentleness with Abby was obvious, his devotion to his aunt undeniable. He moved up the slope with barely contained energy, his long legs keeping a slow, steady pace that exactly matched his aunt's. Thornbushes littered the path and he shoved branches aside, holding them away from Abby's legs. A kind man, it seemed. Though Raven knew better than most how easily a person could hide his true nature.

"Here we are." The slope of the ground eased, and Raven caught her breath at what lay before them—a fenced area contained dozens of gravestones. Some big. Some small. A few towered over the others, immense and beautifully carved with angels and saints.

"This is all one family?"

Shane nodded. "A couple of centuries' worth. It's only been in the past few decades that Meades haven't been buried here."

"Daniel's here." Abby spoke as she opened the wrought-iron gate. "I used to bring flowers every week. Always on Sunday after church. Never missed a week. Even in the snow and rain. I don't remember when I stopped." There was sadness in the words. Knowledge of time passing, of things lost forever.

Raven blinked back the gray edge of melancholy and tried to smile. "This is a beautiful spot. Your ancestors chose well."

"There was a chapel here long ago. Over there—" Abby gestured, frowned. "At least I think it was there. If you look you'll see the foundation stones. And on the other side of the fence, through that back gate, that's where the slaves were buried."

"Slaves?"

"Oh, yes. This was a plantation, after all." Abby walked to a small gravestone. "Look here. See that? A child. Three years old. Never even had a chance at life."

"Aunt Abby, you're being morbid tonight. Let's go home."

"You go. I want to see Daniel. It's been too long." There was an edge to Abby's voice, a fierce expression on her face.

In contrast, Shane's expression was one of tired acceptance. "All right. But then we need to get home."

Raven stayed back as the two wound their way through crumbling stones, allowing Shane and Abby to walk together, sharing whatever memories had brought them here. All around were reminders of life and of death, the people buried here long forgotten, whatever legacy they'd left lost to time and forgetfulness. Raven turned away from the cemetery, choosing instead to look out at the distant gleam of Smith Mountain Lake.

"Where is Daniel's marker? I thought it was under the oak."

Abby spoke loudly, breaking the silence and drawing Raven's attention to the center of the graveyard where Shane and his aunt stood.

Frustration tightened Shane's face, and his features hardened even more. Yet his voice was gentle when he spoke. "There are lots of oak trees around, Aunt Abby."

"The one near the center of the graveyard. Right here. I'm sure of it. Someone's taken the marker down."

Raven tugged at Merry's leash and hurried toward them. "Why don't we look around a little, Abby?"

"No. I'm tired. I just want to see Daniel's gravestone."

"Tell you what, Aunt Abby. You and Raven wait here and I'll look around and see if I can find the right marker. You're sure it was under an oak?"

"Yes. Right near Mother and Daddy."

Shane nodded and turned to Raven. "Do you mind waiting with her? There's a little bench over there."

"No problem. Come on, Abby, let's go sit down."

The wrought-iron bench wasn't made for comfort, but Abby didn't seem to notice. Her gaze was fixed on some distant point, her expression just a little vague.

"Daniel killed himself, you know." The pronouncement was stark, bold, without emotion.

"No. I didn't."

"It was so sad. So terrible. He left four children and his wife behind. And me, of course. We were the last of the Meades. Our children will inherit this land, but I don't think they'll love it like we have."

"How many children do you have?"

"One. Mark."

"Are you close?"

Abby didn't respond. Raven leaned back against the hard bench, her gaze wandering the rows of grave markers, then settling on Shane. He seemed intent on his task, moving quickly from one oak tree to the next, reading the markers, then moving on again.

It should be Abby's son here with her. Not Shane. Raven allowed herself to wonder at the variances of Abby's relationships; that her nephew should be so devoted to her, and her son so much less so seemed odd. But then, Raven knew nothing of the family dynamics that had led them to this place.

A branch snapped behind her and Raven turned. She saw nothing but thickening shadows and tall trees. Still she felt watched, as if someone stood just out of sight, staring hard. Merry seemed to sense the same, her small body tensing, a low growl sounding deep in her throat.

Raven's heart began a hard, erratic beat. Her body stiffened with anxiety. She peered into the shadows, waiting. For what, she didn't know.

"You okay?"

She jumped and whirled around, her pulse subsiding as she spotted Shane. "You startled me."

"Sorry. I was going to call out, but Abby's fallen asleep. I thought I'd let her rest a few minutes."

"Did you find the marker?"

"Yes. Close to the back gate. Near that huge old tree."

"She was right about that, then."

"Not that it'll matter to her. When she wakes up she probably won't remember why we're here. Is there room on that bench?"

Not much. At least not for someone Shane's size. But Raven scooted over anyway.

"Thanks. I'm beat."

"Long day?"

"Not too bad. I've just had a lot of late nights."

"Did you finish writing your book?"

The force of Shane's laughter shook the bench. "Hardly. I've got the Princes of Truth backed into a corner and can't figure out how to get them out of it."

"Princes of Truth? You're Montgomery Wayne?"

"Not if I can't get my characters out of the trouble they're in."

"You will. You're a wonderful storyteller."

"You've read my books?"

"Yes. I'd heard so much about the stories from my Sunday school class, I had to see what they were all about."

"I'm generally more popular with kids than adults."

"I loved the story. I'm not surprised at your success. Have you always been a writer?" The question sounded trite and silly to Raven. Shane had probably been asked it a million times.

Still, he didn't seem to mind answering it. "Not a writer in the truest sense of the word. I'd see a person or an interesting house, even an abandoned car, and be so consumed by the story I made up about it that I'd walk into walls, fall out of chairs, trip over nothing. Used to drive my father nuts."

Raven smiled, imagining a young Shane wandering around with his head in the clouds. "And now that you write books, do you still make up stories about things you see?"

"When something interests me enough. Like you, for instance."

She wasn't sure she liked the direction the conversation was going. "What about me?"

"You're interesting. There are a hundred stories floating through my mind every time I see you."

It was a dare. Raven knew it and was helpless to

back away from the challenge. "All right, I'll bite. What kind of stories?"

"Let's see. How about the one where you're the young wife with the old ogre for a husband. He's hateful and cruel. You're sweet and good. Or the one where you're the fair maiden running from danger, praying for a prince to ride to your rescue."

She laughed to hide her discomfort. "A prince? There are no princes. Just frogs with superiority complexes."

"Now see, that's where you're wrong. There *are* princes. They may be flawed, sometimes horribly so, but their hearts are pure and good, and they'll fight for what's right to their dying breath."

"Like in your books."

"Right." Shane grinned, and Raven felt something inside her melt in response.

She didn't like the feeling. Not at all. "I need to go. I've got a lot to do."

She stood, took a step away.

"Running away, Raven?"

"Not running." Raven turned back, catching her breath at the expression in Shane's eyes. The curiosity. The blatant interest. "Going home."

"What is it about me that makes you nervous?"

"I'm not nervous. I just don't have time to spin tales."

"Too bad. This is the perfect place to do it. Especially now, with the sun just setting and night spilling across the earth." He gestured toward the western horizon, and Raven's gaze followed the movement.

It was just as he'd described it: the sun so low it couldn't be seen, pink and gold shooting toward the east, blue-gray darkness sliding toward the horizon.

Caught in the spell of the sunset, Raven didn't realize Shane had moved until he was beside her, his hand clasping hers. His grip was light but insistent as he tugged her back toward the bench.

"Stay for a little longer. I promise I won't talk about princes, frogs or you."

She couldn't resist, though she told herself she wanted to. "It is nice up here. Even with all the gravestones."

"That's what makes it great. All the people and history that have touched this place. Can't you just imagine a Victorian lady standing on this hill, watching as a loved one was lowered into the ground?"

"I'd rather not."

Shane laughed, the sound ringing out into the quiet evening. "Sorry, I get carried away sometimes. I really appreciate your coming up here with us. Abby's comfortable with you. She's not like that with everyone she meets."

"Things are hard for her right now. Meeting new people just adds to the list of things she's trying to deal with."

"I know. Which is why I've hesitated to bring in fulltime caregivers."

"It will be hard at first, but eventually Abby will adjust."

"She'll adjust more quickly if she has someone she knows, someone she likes with her. Someone like you."

"Me?"

"Why not?"

Raven couldn't think of an answer, so she didn't say anything at all.

"No pressure. I just wanted to throw the idea out."

"Actually, I plan to get a job, but—"

"Then maybe this will work out for both of us. Take a few days, think about it. If you're interested, give me a call."

"I'm interested." The words were out before Raven could think them through.

"Great. Why don't you come by Monday and we'll discuss the details?" He smiled, eyes crinkling at the corners, a dimple creasing his cheek, his expression open and inviting.

Maybe accepting the job wasn't such a good idea after all.

Abby stirred, mumbled something under her breath and straightened, her eyes flying open. "Oh, the cemetery." She struggled up and Shane rose with her, helping her to her feet.

"I've found Daniel's grave. Ready to go see it?"

"Of course. It's been too long."

Raven stood, as well. "It's getting dark. I'd better head home."

"You sure you don't want to come with us? We can walk back to the house together, and Abby and I will give you a ride home."

"Thanks for the offer, but I'll be fine. Come on, Merry." She tugged the puppy's leash and stepped toward the steep hill that led to the lake.

Shane placed a hand on her arm. "Not that way. Straight through to the far gate. See it?"

"Yes."

"The field beyond that leads to the road. Once you get there, turn left. Our driveway is a ten-minute walk. Yours is another fifteen minutes after that. If it gets too dark for you, just stop at our place and I'll give you a ride the rest of the way."

"All right. See you Monday. Goodbye, Abby."

Raven moved through the overgrown cemetery, tugging Merry along beside her. Already dusk had settled on the land and deep violet shadows crept across the ground. The effect was eerie, the rustle of leaves and hum of insects only adding to Raven's unease. She paused with her hand on the gate, thinking she'd go back and wait for Shane and Abby, but when she turned they'd disappeared from view.

Perhaps it was better this way. Relying on others only led to disappointment, and she'd had enough of that to last a lifetime. She pushed open the gate and strode across a wide field, Merry romping close to her feet, undisturbed by Raven's nervousness.

She should take her cue from the dog, let go of the anxiety that strummed through her veins and enjoy the evening. But she couldn't. The cemetery had reminded her too much of life and loss and sorrow. If she'd looked carefully at the gravestones, she would have read names and dates, a short accounting of a person's life. Or a baby's. Raven winced from the thought, not wanting to dwell on the image of mothers standing watch over freshly dug graves.

Her foot snagged on a twisted root and she stumbled, barely caught her balance. With every step the world grew darker, the shadows deeper. A twig snapped somewhere to the right and Merry growled, lunging toward the sound.

"Don't worry. It's just a squirrel." Raven hoped. "Come on, girl, let's hurry." She tugged at the leash and led Merry across grass and weeds and finally onto pavement.

There were no cars on the old country lane. Raven moved toward the middle line, the odd feeling that she was being watched turning her pace to a brisk walk. She passed the Montgomery's driveway, rounded a curve in the road, and spotted the Freedman mailbox.

Home. Finally.

She paused to lift Merry, anxious to hurry the little dog along, and saw a shadow move in the trees beside the road.

"Hello?"

No one answered, and nothing moved in the darkness, yet Raven was sure someone was there. She took a step back, gaze fixed on the edge of the road, and felt the soft rumble of Merry's growl against her chest. She didn't wait for more. Gasping, heart hammering, Raven raced toward the cottage.

Chapter Seven

Raven imagined the sound of feet on gravel behind her, the rasp of someone's breath, a pursuer pressing close to her back. One glance told her no one was there, yet even that didn't ease her fear. She reached the porch at an all-out run and shoved the key into the lock. The door swung open and she stumbled inside, slamming it closed.

It took a moment for her to calm and for her heart to settle back in her chest. When it did, Raven strode to the front window and pulled open the shades, peering out into the darkness. Nothing was there. No one lurked in the yard. She let out a shaky breath and set Merry down on the floor.

"You need to stop growling at shadows, mutt. You almost gave me a heart attack over nothing."

But she pulled the shade down anyway, checking the windows and doors as she moved from room to room. When the phone rang, she jumped, then shook her head at her own skittishness.

"Hello?"

"Raven? It's Shane." Deep and rough, the voice was one Raven would have recognized even if he hadn't given his name.

"Hi, Shane. Is everything okay?"

"Yeah. I'm just checking in, making sure you made it home okay."

Checking on her? It had been years since anyone had cared enough to do that. "I'm fine."

"You sure? You sound a little shaky."

"Just jumping at shadows."

"Shadows?"

"Merry likes to growl at them, and I fall for it every time."

"A guard dog in the making."

"If she doesn't scare us both to death first."

"You want me to come over? Make sure it's just shadows she's growling at?"

Yes. "No, it would be a waste of your time. Thanks for offering, though."

"No problem. You've got my number if you change your mind?"

"Yes."

"Good night, then."

Raven hung up the phone, warmed by his concern, and worried by it. Men were trouble. Especially men like Shane—larger than life, handsome and charming. She'd do well to remember that and keep her distance. Which would be hard if she accepted the job he'd offered her.

But could she refuse it?

Abby needed her, and, truth be told, Raven needed to work. Keeping busy kept her sane, and with Ben out of town, there was little for Raven to do with her time.

She sighed and shook her head. She'd pray about it, see if that gave her a clearer picture of what she should do. For now, she'd occupy herself with other things.

"Come on, Merry, let's go upstairs."

The room at the top of the stairs had once been a bedroom. Now it contained mismatched furniture that Nora had given Raven permission to use. Old bed frames, an end table and a chest crowded one wall. More furniture cluttered the center of the room. She'd move things around, set up a study—anything to keep herself busy. It was that or sit and think.

And there was a lot to think about. Ben and the foster family he loved. Abby and her fading mind. Thea Trebain, missing for years. Daniel, dead by his own hand. Shane.

And Raven's own sad and disappointing past.

She shoved the last thought aside, throwing herself into the job of cleaning the room, working with purpose until she'd cleared a large area. Satisfied with her effort, she turned to a large mirror that stood against one wall. It would be perfect in the living room.

"Get up, mutt. I'm going to move that mirror and you're in the way." Merry didn't move except to roll on her back, her skinny tail wagging.

"I suppose that means something, but since I don't know what, you're going to have to move." Raven leaned down and lifted the puppy, then set her back down a few feet away. "Now stay there. This thing is heavy."

She grunted as she lifted it, stumbling forward under its weight, and felt something give under her foot. Her knee buckled and she went down hard, the mirror still clutched in her hand.

She eased the mirror down and pushed to her feet. A broken board speared up from the floor. She'd have to replace it. Or maybe not. A little wood glue might do the trick. Raven bent forward to take a closer look and was surprised to see a hole beneath the board. Boxed in by wood beams, the space was filled with dust and other things Raven refused to name. And lying amid it all was an old cookie tin.

She lifted it out, grimacing as dead bugs fell off the lid and onto her hands. The weight of the box told her it wasn't empty, though she wasn't expecting what she soon found inside: pearl earrings, a slim gold bracelet, an interesting silver pendant and a small leather diary. Beneath them lay dried flower petals, aged to a delicate hue. Raven ran a finger along one, felt the dryness of it and wondered who they'd been given to.

Perhaps the journal would give her a name. She opened the cover and saw the small, well-formed script: *To Thea. A good and true friend. May this year bring you more happiness than the last and may all your wishes and dreams come true. Happy birthday! With much love, Abby.*

Thea's journal. The urge to read through it was almost overwhelming, but the book and its story belonged to the Trebains. She'd give it to Nora on Sunday. For now, she put the journal back on its bed of petals, replaced the jewelry and closed the box.

Merry yipped and pranced toward the stairs, begging Raven's attention.

"You want to go outside?"

The puppy wagged her ratty tail and scrambled down the steps, Raven right behind her.

Beyond the soft glow of the kitchen light, night lay

heavy and black. Raven stared out into the darkness, unease curling in her belly as she pulled the door open and let Merry out. Maybe the stillness and silence of rural life was wearing on her. How else to explain the vulnerability she felt as she stood silhouetted in the doorway?

"Come on, Merry. Hurry up."

The puppy raced back into the house and Raven slammed the door, shutting out the night and whatever secrets it held.

Sunday-morning sun burst through the slats in the blinds, burning away the nightmares that had haunted Raven's sleep for the past two nights. She rose and showered, then dressed quickly, glad to be going to church. Happy to have something to do. Memories dogged her waking hours, nightmares haunted her sleep, and it showed in the pale cast of her skin and the deep circles under her eyes.

She yanked uncooperative hair into a barrette and applied light makeup. No earrings or necklace, nothing to draw attention to herself, though she did take a thin silver anklet from her jewelry box and clasp it around her ankle. Then she examined herself critically. The suit was lilac colored, but conservative, the skirt skimming the top of her knees. The jacket was trim but not tight. She looked like the doctor's wife she'd once been—classically elegant, everything understated but chic.

She hated it.

Hopefully it would be just the right thing for a pastor's sister to wear. Raven sighed, grabbed the cookie tin from the table and opened the door, nudging Merry away when the dog tried to bound outside.

"Sorry, pup. You've been out already. Be good and when I get home I'll take you for a long walk."

She shut the door firmly, trying to ignore the loud wails that followed her departure.

She'd never been one for crowded places and Grace Christian was that and more, the hallway filled with people talking and chatting before the service, the sanctuary just as full. She smiled at people as she made her way along the aisle, hoping they couldn't see how uncomfortable she really was.

"Raven! I was hoping you'd show up." Nora Freedman shoved her way through the throng.

"Nora. Good morning."

"It is, isn't it? Though I'd say it would be a mite better if Ben were here to preach, what with this being your first week at church."

"I don't mind."

"Of course you don't. Come on. You can sit with me and the other ladies. Widows and old maids, all of us."

She led Raven to the front of the church, gesturing to a pew where several women sat. Three men were squeezed in among them. One was Sam Riley. He looked up and winked as Raven slid into the pew. Nora shook her head and whispered loud enough for the entire church to hear.

"That man should be shot for convincing you to take a scrappy little mongrel. I heard all about it from Lulu. She works at the veterinary clinic."

"You did say I could have pets?"

"Of course. I just didn't think that fiend would get you to take one of his. Go on now, scoot in there next to Reena."

Raven did as she was told. It was so much easier to

float with the tide than to struggle against it. By the time the organ music began she was neatly sandwiched between Reena Bradley, a plain-faced, rather dour woman, and Nora. It might have been comfortable if the former hadn't doused herself in perfume. Raven's nose itched, her eyes watered and she was sure she'd start sneezing at any moment.

"Are you all right?" Nora spoke quietly this time, perhaps mistaking Raven's watering eyes for tear-filled ones.

"Perfume has this effect on me." she whispered, not wanting to offend Reena.

"Oh, you poor thing. Do you want to move? I'd be happy to go with you."

Raven shook her head, sneezed, and fumbled in her bag for a tissue. Someone behind her dangled one over her shoulder, and Raven grabbed it.

"Thanks."

"No problem."

Raven knew the voice. Was surprised she hadn't noticed when he walked in. She turned to meet Shane's gaze.

"Good morning, Shane. Abby."

Shane smiled, but Abby stared straight ahead, as if unaware of the greeting.

"Is Abby doing okay this morning?"

"It hasn't been a good one, if that's what you're asking." He sounded tired and his eyes flashed with frustration.

"Anything I can do?"

"We're okay for now. I don't think you've met Abby's son, Mark, or his wife, Laura." He gestured to the couple sitting on Abby's other side. "Mark, Laura. This is Raven Stevenson—the nurse I was telling you about."

"And I'm Adam Meade. Abby's nephew." A slim, handsome man slid into the pew, smiling at Raven, though his eyes seemed cold.

Raven opened her mouth to respond and sneezed instead.

Adam jerked back, and Shane's lips quirked. His eyes danced with humor as he handed Raven another tissue. "Allergies?"

"I'm afraid so." She turned to Nora. "I *am* going to have to move. I'll catch up with you after the service. I've got a few things in my car that I want to give you. A diary and some jewelry that belonged to Thea."

"A diary. How wonderful. I'm sure her family would love to have it."

"Great. I'll look for you after the service." Raven stood and gathered her Bible and purse, pausing when Shane spoke from behind her.

"Abby and I should probably sit closer to the back, just in case we need to leave early. Why don't the three of us go together?"

"No, I—"

But the decision was already made. Nora stood, smiling at Shane. "Now that's a sensible idea. I'll see you after the service, Raven."

It took a minute to get Abby moving, and by the time Shane managed it, Raven was already seated in the last pew. It was a good choice—one Shane would have made himself if he hadn't wanted to give Abby a chance to sit with her son. A son who hadn't said more than a word to his mother since they'd arrived.

He shrugged off irritation and helped Abby situate herself, then slid into the pew beside her, glancing toward Raven in time to catch her stare. Her cheeks flushed, the tinge of color adding a soft glow to her skin as she turned away. She looked professional today, no longer the flower child Shane had first encountered. Too bad. Wild hair and flowing dresses suited her. Though he had to admit, she looked just as good in a trim suit and tied-back hair.

Despite his best efforts to concentrate on the sermon, Shane found his gaze drawn to Raven again and again. She shifted, as if aware of his attention, and he caught a glint of silver at her ankle. An ankle bracelet? Shane leaned closer, wanting to get a better look, and was brought up short by an elbow to his ribs.

He turned, saw the granite profile of the county sheriff, and wondered if the elbow had been an accident, or a warning. He suspected the latter, as he'd heard Jake and Ben were good friends. Whatever the case, Shane figured he'd deserved the elbow. After all, he had been staring at Raven, just as he stared at other people he found interesting. It was a bad habit of his, one he wasn't always successful at curbing.

The sermon wound to an end before Shane could get his mind back where it belonged. He blamed the lapse on fatigue. The past few nights had been rough, Abby's behavior difficult. Tomorrow he'd speak with Raven, decide the best course of action in regard to Abby's care. Until then he'd just have to make do. He turned toward Raven, wanting to ask what time she planned to stop by in the morning, and caught a glimpse of her lilac-colored suit as she hurried away.

"Shane Montgomery, right?"

Shane bit back a sigh as he turned to face the sheriff. "That's right."

"I'm Jake Reed. This is my wife, Tiffany."

A tall redhead leaned around Jake and shook Shane's hand. "It's nice to finally meet you, Shane. I've read several of your books."

"I hope you enjoyed them."

"I did. Though I probably shouldn't admit it, since they're written for a younger audience. Sorry to say hi and run, but I've got a meeting in a few minutes." She planted a kiss on her husband's cheek and hurried away.

Which left Shane and the sheriff.

"Nice meeting you, Jake. I've got to get Abby home, so if you'll excuse me…"

"She looks like she's having fun. Seems a shame to make her leave now."

Shane glanced at his aunt. Sure enough, she was surrounded by friends and looked happy. Which was too bad, as Jake seemed to have something on his mind. Something Shane felt confident he didn't want to hear.

"You're right. What can I do for you?"

"Just wondering what's going on between you and Raven."

"Guess I'm wondering why that's your business."

"Ben's a good friend. I've made it my business to look out for his sister while he's gone."

"I don't think she'd appreciate it."

"She doesn't have to know."

"But I do?"

"Maybe. Ben said she's had a rough time. I wouldn't want things to get rougher while she's here."

"If they do, it won't be because of me. I've hired her to work with Abby. Should be a good arrangement for both of us."

"Let's hope so. Gotta go. Take care of your aunt."

"Ready, Aunt Abby?" Shane led Abby from the sanctuary, his mind circling back to Raven again.

Jake's comments had been interesting, hinting at a difficult past. It wasn't hard to imagine they were true. He pictured Raven—strong hands and thin body, determined and compassionate spirit, eyes that spoke of sadness and disillusion. She'd been hurt before. No doubt about it. But she wouldn't be again. Not if Shane had anything to do with it.

Chapter Eight

Running from the sanctuary had been a silly and childish thing to do, and Raven didn't bother denying the fact as she hurried across the church parking lot. Shane made her uncomfortable, his intense gaze reminding her of all the things she once wanted, but now told herself she no longer needed. After all, love and marriage weren't all they were cracked up to be. She knew that, had lived the nightmare of it. She wouldn't repeat the mistake.

Images ran through her mind, memories of Jonas—handsome, charming, smiling as he promised to love and cherish her forever. His forever had lasted a few days. Then he'd decided to "fix" Raven's imperfections. For a while she'd allowed herself to be molded into the sophisticated, soft-spoken, trophy wife he'd wanted, but even then, it hadn't been enough. With Jonas nothing had ever been enough.

She pushed back the memories and leaned into the car to get the cookie tin she'd brought for Nora.

"Need some help?"

Raven jumped, bumping her head on the roof of the car, and turned to face Shane and Abby. "You startled me."

"Sorry." Shane didn't look sorry as he reached to help her. He looked amused.

What was it about the man that made her want to return his grin, relax her guard and allow herself to enjoy the moment? "Abby looks tired. Are you taking her home?"

"Trying to rush me away, Raven?"

She ignored the question, turning to face Abby. "You look lovely today, Abby."

"Thank you, dear. Have we met?"

"I'm Raven."

"That's an interesting name. Where did you get it?"

"My mother saw a black bird outside the hospital window the day I was born. Since she hadn't decided on a name, that's what she called me."

"Nice."

Raven didn't acknowledge Shane's comment. She'd gotten past the story of her name long ago. "I've got to go find Nora. I have some things to give her."

"Before you go, we need to pick a time for our meeting tomorrow."

"Does nine work for you?"

"Sounds good to me. We'll see you then."

"All right. Bye." She turned toward the church, expecting Shane to move away.

Instead he leaned close and spoke into her ear. "I like that ankle bracelet you're wearing. I'm thinking maybe the princess in my story should have one."

He winked, stepped back and ushered Abby away.

Raven didn't realize she was smiling until they'd disappeared from view. She didn't want to be amused by Shane, didn't want to be pulled into his easy humor and knowing gaze. Doing so could only lead to hurt, and she'd been hurt enough for one lifetime.

The church hall was almost empty, the sound of Raven's heels echoing on the tile floor. A few people mingled in the sanctuary, and Raven could feel curious gazes as she stepped inside and looked for Nora. She wasn't there. Raven would have to call and make arrangements to bring her the box.

"Ms. Stevenson?"

Raven turned to face the speaker, a smile of greeting in place. "Mr. Montgomery, it's nice to see you again."

"If you have a minute I'd like to speak with you. I have a few questions regarding my mother's care."

"Sure."

"There's an empty room around the corner. Why don't we go there?"

He didn't bother to close the door and barely waited for Raven to clear the threshold before he began. "I want to know what your interest in my mother is."

"I'm a nurse. Abby is going to be my patient."

"And?"

"And nothing. I'm trained in geriatrics. I've been working in the home health-care industry for three years. I need a job. Shane offered me one."

"So it's just a coincidence that you look like an old friend of my mother's. One she misses desperately?"

"What else would it be?"

"A deliberate act. One designed to make you indispensable to an elderly woman who is obviously losing the ability to make rational judgments."

"I'm not sure where you're going with this, Mr. Montgomery."

"Then I'll be blunt. My mother is a wealthy woman. If you think you're going to get some of her money—"

"I'm here for my brother. Nothing more or less than that." Anger colored the words and she did nothing to hide it.

"I can't know that."

"If you're uncomfortable with the situation, I'd rather not take the job. Tell Shane he'll need to find someone else."

She planned to walk away, but he placed a hand on her arm, all his anger seemingly gone. "I'm sorry. I was out of line."

"Yes. You were."

A half smile eased the tension in his face. "Glad to see we agree."

"Actually, we don't. You've made a lot of assumptions about me that aren't very flattering, Mr. Montgomery."

"Mark. And you're right. I should have checked things out before I spoke with you. But my cousin, Adam, called me last night, said Abby was talking about Thea Trebain. I've seen pictures. There's a marked resemblance between the two of you."

"And you thought I'd planned it that way?"

"My mother is vulnerable right now. I don't want her hurt."

"Check out my references. If you're not satisfied, then let me know and I'll back off from the job." Despite her irritation Raven dug in her bag for a pen and piece of paper, and wrote down the names. She handed him the list.

"Thanks. Like I said, I'm sorry for jumping the gun on things."

"I understand."

"Probably not, but thanks for saying so." With that, he turned and walked away.

Raven hurried outside to her car. Mark Montgomery was a difficult man, but she shouldn't let it bother her. She'd dealt with plenty of difficult people in her life. She had lived with a man who was more than difficult—Jonas had been angry, confrontational, determined to have his way in everything. Compared to that, dealing with Mark would be a piece of cake.

But what about dealing with Shane? She couldn't stop the question from whispering through her mind. Shane wasn't difficult, but he was dangerous in other ways. Ways Raven didn't want to acknowledge.

He'd made her smile.

That worried her. She didn't *want* to like Shane. Not when she knew there was something more than like between them. There was attraction. A deep, gut-level response to one another that begged to be explored. And that was something Raven couldn't let happen.

She'd just have to be careful, focus on Abby, do the job she was paid for, but not allow herself to be pulled into the family, or closer to Shane.

It was a good plan. So why did she have a feeling things weren't going to turn out as she intended them to? Maybe because things never turned out the way she planned.

But God was in control, right?

The thought wasn't as comforting as it should have been. Raven shook her head as she got in the car and started it. She'd go home, take Merry for a run, have a cup of herbal tea and force herself to stop worrying.

Even after her run, even while she sat on the sofa, a cup of steaming tea in her hand, Raven couldn't shake the anxiety that thrummed along her nerves. She knew the reason. *The cemetery.* It had been haunting her mind since she'd been there with Abby and Shane. The worn, faded stones that chronicled the lives of the babies and children who'd died, crying out to her in her dreams, sliding into her mind as she moved through the day. Reminding her of what she'd lost.

It shouldn't hurt so much. Not after five years. But it did. Micah had been everything she'd longed for. A little boy to cherish, a family, love.

And gone before she even had a chance to know him.

Merry whined and nudged her nose against Raven's leg, as if sensing her distress.

"Don't worry. I'm all right."

Sometimes.

But not today.

She walked into the bedroom and opened her jewelry box, pulled out a silver locket. It felt heavy in her hands as she pressed the clasp and eased it open to see the photo. Micah as he'd been minutes after his birth—tiny, perfectly formed, a miniature version of the full-term baby he would never be. Her throat was tight with tears she refused to shed, afraid if she let them start she'd never stop. At twenty-three weeks he'd been too little to survive, yet she'd held him, pulled his tiny body to her, felt the minute bones, the shallow breaths, the moment his soul had eased away.

"I miss you, sweetie." She traced the image with her fingernail, then slowly closed the locket again.

Shane was at the end of his rope. So were the Princes of Truth. Maybe he should let them be devoured by the Lie Beast. At least then he wouldn't have to worry about deadlines. He reread the paragraph he'd just written, deleted it, and prayed for inspiration. He'd need it if he was to get the manuscript finished on time.

The phone rang and he picked it up, more glad than frustrated by the interruption. "Hello?"

"Abby thinks I'm poisoning her. She's knocked all the food off the table and has herself locked in the bathroom. You need to come do something."

Shane wanted to refuse, but if Kaylee was calling the office and interrupting his writing time it had to be just as serious as she said. "I'm coming."

Kaylee was in the kitchen scrubbing at her shirt when he stepped into the room. She looked up and grimaced. "Upstairs bathroom. Master suite. She's shouting for the police."

"What'd you try to feed her?"

"Soup. Chicken noodle. I thought it was innocuous enough."

"It isn't your fault."

"Maybe not. But I feel terrible about it. Abby and I were getting along so well."

"I'll go get her."

It took fifteen minutes to convince Abby to come out. By the time Shane managed it he was out of patience, but was careful to conceal his frustration as he led her from the room.

"Want an omelet?"

"I'm not hungry."

"You sure?"

"All the food's poisoned. Just ask Thea. She'll tell you."

"Aunt Abby, you're not being poisoned. You've known Kaylee for years. She adores you."

"People change."

Shane sighed and decided against arguing. "You need to eat. You're fading away to nothing."

"So? What does it matter?" The words were stark and filled with sorrow.

"It matters a lot. I don't want you to waste away."

"I'm already doing that. There's nothing to stop it."

"Aunt Abby—"

"I'm hungry." And just like that the moment was over.

"Why don't I make you something?"

"Bread."

"Great. We've got a loaf downstairs."

"No. Not the kind in the can. The other kind."

Shane bit back impatience, knowing Abby couldn't help her mistakes. "You mean you want another kind of bread? Wheat? Rye?"

"The kind we make ourselves."

"I know nothing about baking, Aunt Abby, so I'm afraid you're out of luck."

A tear slid down her cheek, puddling in the lines there. Shane felt something tug at his heart.

"Maybe Kaylee knows how to bake bread."

"Not Kaylee. Thea and I bake bread together. I'll go visit her and see if she wants to help." The tears were still falling, as if a piece of Abby's mind was silently mourning what she was losing.

"Why don't I call her?"

"I can."

"Aunt Abby…" But what could he do? Refuse to let her use the phone? Refuse to let her make decisions about what she wanted and didn't want? "Do you know the number?"

"I don't know."

"Maybe we should invite her another day."

"But that might be too late. I'll call 911 and get her number."

"411, Aunt Abby. And don't bother. I have her number. Here, I'll dial. You talk."

The phone rang as Raven stepped into the kitchen. She picked it up, glad for the distraction. "Hello?"

"Thea?"

Raven tensed at the name. Then the voice registered, and she relaxed. "Abby."

"I've missed you so much."

"I've missed you, too."

"Then come by today. We'll bake bread like we used to."

"I don't know, Abby—"

"We haven't visited in ages." The tears in Abby's voice stole Raven's choice.

"I'll be there soon."

Bread baking? There was a first time for everything, she supposed.

The kitchen was at the back of the Montgomery house and Raven knocked on that door, hoping Abby or her caregiver would answer. Instead, Shane opened the door, his broad shoulders blocking her view of the room, his green eyes taking in her shower-wet hair and makeup-free face.

"Now this is more what I'm use to."

"What? Messy hair?"

"No, the flower child look. Wild hair and long, flowing dress."

"I was in a hurry."

"There was no rush. Abby doesn't keep track of time."

"Next time I'll be sure to put my hair up."

"Hopefully not on my account. I like it this way." He

put a hand on Raven's arm, stopping her when she would have slid past him. "Were you rushing to get to Abby? Or were you running from whatever it is I see in your eyes?"

Startled, Raven pulled back, uncomfortable with how easily he could read her, wanting to walk away before he could see more of who she was.

"Don't worry, I won't ask any more questions. Come on in. Abby's in the parlor with her caregiver." Then he stepped aside and let her move past.

Broken glass littered the floor. Bits of food and spilled milk pooled beneath the table. A loaf of bread had been ripped to shreds and lay in wet lumps.

"What happened?"

"Abby thinks she's being poisoned."

"Does she realize what she's done?"

"I don't think so. That's why she's in the parlor. I want to get this cleaned up before she bakes her bread."

"I'll help."

"No. Go see Abby. I'll finish up in here."

"Four hands are better than two."

"I thought it was two hands are better than one?"

"Not in this case." Raven grabbed a broom that had been abandoned against the refrigerator and began sweeping clumps of food and muck into a pile.

Shane thought he should argue. After all, Raven was a nurse, not a maid, but she worked so much more efficiently than he did, sweeping in smooth productive motions, her arms toned and capable despite her thinness, that he decided it might be better to let her help.

"I thought we were going to work together?" She'd paused in her sweeping, and eyed him with a mixture of amusement and frustration.

"Sorry. Bad habit." Shane grabbed a plastic trash bag and began throwing pieces of broken glass inside.

"Staring at people is a bad habit? Or letting other people do your work?"

"Staring at people. I usually don't like people around when I'm working. Complicates things." Shane spoke as he reached down to grab the broken teacup. His arm brushed Raven's calf.

Raven must have noticed. She'd stopped sweeping again and was staring down at him, her eyes wide with surprise and the same fear Shane had noticed before. He wanted to ask what had put it there, but he didn't have time. A flurry of activity in the hall warned him a moment before Abby burst into the room with Kaylee right behind her.

"I'm sorry, Shane. She—"

"Shane Montgomery, what have you done?"

"Just a little accident, Aunt Abby."

"An accident?" Then her attention drifted away and she was looking at Raven, a wide smile creasing her face. "Oh, you came. I thought you'd forgotten. We're making toast today."

"I'm looking forward to it, Abby. First I'll help Shane clean up this mess."

"Mess?" Abby glanced around the room. "Oh dear, what happened?"

Raven was sure she heard Shane sigh, but he hid his exasperation well.

"Just a little accident, Aunt Abby. Why don't you sit down here while we finish up?"

"Yes. I think I will." She allowed herself to be helped into the chair. "I wonder if I could have some tea."

"I'll get it for you, Abby." The fair-haired woman who'd followed Abby into the kitchen hurried to the stove and started the burner, then turned to smile at Raven. "I'm Kaylee, by the way, since Shane's head is too far in the clouds for him to bother with introductions."

"Raven Stevenson."

"I heard you moved into the Freedman property."

"You and everyone else in town." Raven grinned to take the sting out of the words, and Kaylee nodded.

"That's part of life here. How do you like Lakeview so far?"

"It's nice."

"And will you be staying long?"

"For a while. I'm here to visit my brother. Ben Avery." Raven began sweeping again, aware that Kaylee wasn't the only one listening.

Shane was picking up large pieces of glass and food and dropping them into the bag, but his focus was on her, not the job. He met her gaze and smiled. "Don't stop talking on my account."

"Don't stop working on mine."

Shane laughed, the sound deep and full. It shivered along Raven's spine and made her wonder what her reaction to him would be like if she hadn't married Jonas. If she didn't have so much in her life to regret.

"Here's your tea, Abby." Kaylee's voice cut through Raven's thoughts and she forced her mind back to cleaning.

It didn't take long to finish the job. Kaylee pitched in, mopping the floor while Raven wiped the table and Shane carried the garbage bag outside.

"I've got to head out. Can you tell Shane I'll be happy to fill in again if he needs me?"

"I'll tell him."

"Are we going to can the beans now?"

Raven glanced at Abby, saw that she'd finished her tea and was staring into the distance. "Beans?"

"Or is it baking day? I've forgotten."

"Baking day. Shall we make some bread?"

"What a wonderful idea. There's yeast in the refrigerator, I think. Would you mind checking…I'm sorry, I've forgotten your name."

"Raven."

"That's right. Raven. You look a lot like an old friend of mine. Thea. She had the same curly hair and the same thin frame. I always envied that about her."

"You were good friends?"

"Oh, yes, the best. Father didn't like it, but Mother was a sweet woman, way ahead of her time. She didn't care that Thea was black, or that her mother wasn't married."

"She sounds like a great lady."

"Who?" Shane asked as he stepped back into the room.

"Abby's mother."

"From what I heard, she was. I never met her. She died when Abby was in her early teens, I think. Is that right, Abby?"

"I'm the only one left now. Sometimes it seems like a dream, and I wonder if I just imagined it all. I need to find the book, but I can't remember where I left it…" Her voice trailed off and she stepped toward the back door, tears sliding down her cheeks.

"Where are you going, Aunt Abby?" Shane slid an arm around her shoulders, his expression somber, his voice gentle.

Raven's heart broke a little at the sight they made—the tall, sturdy man and the fragile, fading woman.

Tears pricked her eyes, and she turned away, reaching for the flour and sugar she'd placed on the counter. "Maybe we should put this away for now."

"You still up for baking bread, Aunt Abby? Or do you want to do this another day?"

"That's right, we were baking. Do we have raisins?" She stepped back to the counter, forgetting for the moment, it seemed, whatever had upset her.

"Top shelf on the left."

Raven opened the cupboard and found the unopened box just where Shane had said it would be. "Here we are. Raisins."

"Good. Looks like we're ready to bake."

"Abby and I are ready. You can go write."

"No way. Abby's caregiver won't be here until five. I'm here until then."

"I'll stay with her. Go write."

"Yes, Shane. Go. You're very irritating in the kitchen. And clumsy. Look at the mess we just had to clean up because of you."

Shane snorted at that, and opened his mouth to argue. Raven didn't give him the chance.

"You're wasting writing time."

"I'm beginning to think I'm not wanted around here." He smiled and kissed his aunt on the cheek. Then he tugged one of Raven's curls. "Keep her out of trouble. If you need me, call me at the office. The number is by the phone."

He left then, and Raven set to work, trying not to notice how empty the room felt without him.

Chapter Nine

Half an hour later a ball of sticky, raisin-studded dough sat in a covered bowl on the counter. According to the recipe it would need to rise for another forty minutes before it could be shaped. If it rose at all.

Raven wasn't sure it would, as Abby had added a few ingredients that weren't listed in the recipe. She didn't share her misgivings, just smiled at Abby who sat sipping tea and looking quite pleased with their accomplishment.

"Well, that's that. Maybe we should take a walk while we wait for it to rise."

"That would be lovely, dear."

"I'll call Shane and let him know where we're going."

It took only a moment to check with Shane and get Abby ready for the stroll. "Shall we go to the road? Or walk through the field."

"Are we going to the cottage?" Abby asked.

"I hadn't thought of it, but if you'd like to, we can. I need to let my puppy out anyway."

The day had warmed a bit, the sun streaming through tall trees and bathing the ground with gold as they walked.

They reached the cottage easily and Raven helped Abby up onto the porch steps. Then she opened the door to let Merry out. The puppy was ecstatic, leaping and bounding across the yard, and only returning to the house when Raven picked her up and carried her there.

Abby didn't respond to the puppy, nor did she speak when Raven helped her to her feet and led her back toward the Montgomery property. They were almost to the mailbox when they heard an engine roar. Raven turned toward the sound and saw a car careening around the curve in the road.

"Watch out, this car's coming fast."

And straight toward them!

Heart thundering, mouth dry with fear, Raven leaped to the side of the road, pushing Abby behind a tree and scrambling to follow. Tires squealed, brakes screeched. Then the world exploded.

Someone was screaming, Shane could hear it through the open window. He bolted out of his chair and raced from the office. He took the steps two at a time, adrenaline pumping through him as the screams continued. It sounded like Abby.

He'd almost reached the road when she stumbled into view, still shrieking, terror making her eyes wide.

"Hurry! Hurry!"

"What happened? Where's Raven?"

"Hurry!"

They moved as quickly as Abby could. Much too slowly for Shane, clearing the driveway, stepping onto the road. That's when he saw the car. Bright red, gleaming in the fading light, it was half on, half off the road, its hood crumpled against a tree. The engine was still running, the door left opened.

"Raven!" Shane shouted as he sprinted toward the wreck.

"I'm okay." The words were barely audible to Shane above the sound of his pounding heart. He might have thought he'd imagined them if Raven hadn't stepped into view.

Blood dripped from a wound on her head. Her hem was torn, the fabric ragged and hanging open; both her knees were raw and weeping blood.

"Don't move." Shane barked the order as he ran toward her, praying she'd listen.

She did, standing still until he was beside her; staying quiet as he lifted her into his arms. He turned to his aunt, saw that she was pale and shaken, but still upright, still aware.

"Come on, Abby. We need to get her back to the house."

Raven meant to protest, meant to tell Shane she'd been hurt a lot worse in her life, but her mouth wouldn't cooperate with her mind. Worse, her body had betrayed her, leaning into Shane's warmth, gathering strength from the fast, steady beat of his heart. She closed her eyes, then opened them again and found herself lying on a couch, Shane and Abby standing over her.

"I'm fine." But even as she spoke the words, Raven was cataloguing her injuries, trying to decide how hurt she really was.

Shane pressed a hand against her shoulder. "Lie back. You've got a head injury."

"Just a cut, I think." Raven raised a shaky hand to her head, fingering a jagged tear near her hairline. It wasn't bad. Not nearly as bad as it could have been. "Nothing that won't heal on its own."

"The ambulance will be here in a few minutes. I called the sheriff, too."

"Good, but I don't need an ambulance."

"Let's let them decide."

Shane was running roughshod over Raven and she didn't like it. She'd lived too many years under Jonas's thumb to ever let another man tell her what to do. She sat up, ignoring a twinge of pain in her side.

"How about Abby? Is she all right?"

"There's not a scratch on her."

"Guess we were both pretty lucky, weren't we, Abby."

But Abby was sitting in the reclining chair, staring toward the window. She looked lost and lonely, her white hair in disarray, her sweater covered with grass stains and twigs. Raven wanted to go to her, to put an arm around her shoulder, ask where she'd gone and try to find a way to pull her back.

"Abby—" She tried to stand, but Shane pressed a hand against her shoulder again.

"For crying out loud, Raven. You were hit by a car. Lie back."

"I'm okay." But the world was spinning, rushing toward her in a hodgepodge of color.

"Sure you are." Shane eased her down against the cushions as he spoke, and Raven allowed him to do it.

"I am. The car didn't hit me. It hit a tree."

"Yeah? Then how'd you end up with a cut head and wrecked knees?"

"I think I tripped."

"Right. I hear the sirens. Stay put."

It wasn't a request, and Raven had no intention of

complying. But her head felt heavy, her eyes tired, and a slow throb was working its way up her leg. She bit back a groan and settled back on the couch.

Commotion near the door drew Raven's attention away from the pain. She glanced toward the sound, watching as Shane walked back into the room, a tall, heavyset man beside him.

"Raven, this is Ted Marshal. He's from the Sheriff's Department. Ted, Raven Stevenson."

The officer stepped forward, his gaze traveling from Raven's blood-soaked hair to her torn knees. "Already checked out the accident site. Looks like you had a close call out there. Did you see the driver of the car?"

"No. Everything happened too fast."

"Not even a vague impression?"

Raven thought back and could remember only blurs of color and motion. "Nothing."

"Too bad. The car went missing from a car dealership in Lynchburg last night or early this morning."

"You think it's a kid?" Shane spoke as he leaned toward Raven and wrapped a hand around hers, smoothing his thumb over her clenched fingers and knuckles.

The officer didn't seem to notice, and just went on with his thoughts. "Probably. It happens all the time. Kid gets dared, steals a car, drives it around for a while and leaves it on a back road for the police to find and return."

"Only this time he didn't know how to drive and wrecked it?"

"Like I said. It happens. And this time the kid was lucky. Lots of times it isn't just the car that's damaged."

"And it *isn't* just the car this time." Shane's voice was quiet, though his anger was obvious.

A look passed between the two men, a lifetime of hostility exchanged without a word.

Raven spoke into the tension. "Luckily no permanent damage was done."

Shane shot her a look, squeezed her hand lightly. "You're right. I hear the ambulance. I'll go show them in."

He released Raven's hand and stepped away. She thought of calling out to him. Of telling him she'd rather he stay and let the officer take care of the ambulance. She didn't. That would have made her feel weak and needy—two character flaws she'd worked hard to overcome. Instead she forced herself up and walked over to Abby, wincing only a little as the movement jarred her head.

"Are you okay, Abby?"

The older woman turned as Raven spoke. There were tears on her cheeks, drying but still obvious. "Oh, you poor thing. How could I have let this happen?"

"You didn't let anything happen. It was an accident. Some kid taking a joyride."

"Was it? I wasn't sure."

"Of course it was."

But something nudged at the edges of Raven's mind. Something that didn't fit but that was too vague to put her finger on. Now wasn't the time to think about it, not with Abby so clearly upset.

Raven put a hand on her shoulder. "Nothing that happened today was your fault."

She might have said more, but Shane walked back into the room, the ambulance crew behind him. His gaze went from the couch to Raven and he quirked a brow.

"Why did I know you would be up taking care of Abby instead of lying down taking care of yourself?"

"I just wanted to be sure she was all right."

"Now it's your turn." He put his hand under her elbow and led her back to the couch.

"This is silly. I'm shaken, but not badly hurt."

"Why don't you let us take a look, ma'am?" A young man, no more than twenty-two, stepped toward her and Raven decided not to fight the inevitable.

She allowed herself to be poked and prodded, cleaned and bandaged, but refused to go to the hospital. She'd spent too much time in one after Micah's birth and again at the end of Jonas's illness. She had no intention of being in one again. Not if she could help it.

"You won't need stitches." The attendant swabbed her forehead one last time. "But see your doctor as soon as possible."

"I will."

"And go to the emergency room if you have shortness of breath, dizziness or blurred vision. You said you were a nurse, so I'm sure you know the drill." He packed up the medical kit he'd been using and smiled at Raven. "You're new in town, right?"

"I moved in a week ago."

"I didn't think I'd seen you before. I'm Rick. It's nice to meet you. Too bad it wasn't under better circumstances. We'll have to try this again when you're feeling better."

Raven blinked. Was he hinting that he'd like to see her again? She'd been out of the dating game for far too long to know the cues. Since she wasn't particularly interested in learning them, she played dumb.

"I'm sure you meet lots of people this way."

"Not as many as you might think. We're heading out. Take care."

"Looks like you've got a fan." Shane whispered the

words in her ear, then followed the emergency crew outside.

"Glad to hear you're going to be okay, Ms. Stevenson."

She'd forgotten about the officer, and now turned to face him. He leaned against the wall, his arms crossed.

"Thanks. Do you think you'll find the driver?"

"Maybe. We'll dust for prints. See if we get a match. Sometimes we get lucky." He shrugged. "There something going on between you and Montgomery?"

"Is that question relevant?"

"Montgomery's a troublemaker. Don't know why he bothered coming back to Lakeview. Abby'd be better off without him."

"Isn't that up to her to decide?"

Marshal leaned down, his face so close to Raven's she could see every pore in his skin. She refused to back away—just stared back with the same intensity he was shooting at her.

When he finally spoke, his words were quiet, barely audible. "Ms. Abby isn't in a position to judge something like that. You're a nurse. You can see what's happening here. An old woman being taken advantage of. Montgomery moved in here a couple months ago. He lives in her house, eats her food, has access to her money. What's she get in the bargain? An attempt on her life."

"You said—"

"I said kids. Probably was kids. But maybe not."

"He'd never hurt Abby."

"You don't know him well, do you? He's got a reputation. One he earned. Ask around." He straightened, backed up. "I'm going to dust for prints on the car. Get the paperwork filed. If we find anything out, we'll give

you a holler. You have any questions, give me a call."
He passed her a business card and stalked out.

"You sure you don't want to go to the hospital?"
Shane spoke from the doorway, his hair mussed as if
he'd run his hands through it over and over again, his
gaze the same as always—intent, curious.

"I'm sure. There's nothing wrong with me that a little rest won't cure."

"All right. Give me a minute to call Abby's doctor
and I'll give you a ride home."

"I can walk."

"Sure you can walk. You might even be able to run.
But is that the best choice? You're a nurse. What would
you tell someone with your injuries?"

To call a doctor. To rest. To let other people take care
of her for a while. "I'll take the ride."

But nothing else. Not from Shane. Not from anyone.
Not as long as she was healthy and strong enough to take
care of herself.

Shane placed the call. Then turned back to Raven.
"The doctor's coming by in a few minutes to check
Abby. After that I can make a run to the store if you need
aspirin or bandages."

"Thanks, but I'm a nurse. My house is fully stocked
for emergencies."

"I'll keep that in mind."

"Why? Do you have lots of emergencies that need
medical attention?"

"Not as many as I used to."

"Good. I think there's been enough excitement
around here for a while."

"'Excitement' is putting it mildly. Marshal is convinced the accident was a teen prank. I'm not so sure."

"Why do you say that?"

"Seems odd that the kid made it from Lynchburg to Lakeview before he smashed into a tree. That's a thirty-minute drive on well-traveled roads."

"Maybe seeing me and Abby on an empty road scared him and he lost control."

"Maybe. Could be my imagination is making more of the situation than there is. It's happened before."

"If it wasn't an accident, then what?"

"Good question. One I don't have an answer to."

"I'm sure it's exactly what it seems." But even as she denied it, Raven couldn't help wondering if Shane was right…if the accident had been something more sinister than a joyride gone wrong.

Chapter Ten

Three days' recuperation was enough, and on Wednesday, despite both Ben's and Shane's protests, Raven decided it was time to meet with Shane and discuss her new job. When Ben phoned early that morning, she was already dressed and ready to go.

"You sound wide-awake."

"I am. No sense sleeping the day away."

"Didn't the doctor tell you to rest?"

"I did."

"We had this conversation yesterday, remember? We agreed you wouldn't be ready to work until next week."

"We didn't agree. You gave me your opinion. I respect it, but the decision is mine to make. And I've decided I'm ready to work."

There was silence, then a sigh. "Sometimes it's okay to let other people look out for you, Rae."

"When I need someone to take care of me, I'll let it happen. Right now, I'm fine."

"Just don't push yourself."

"I won't. I know my limitations."

"Do you?"

Ben's question echoed through Raven's mind as she let Merry out, watered the plants, made her bed. It was still echoing there as she walked across the field and over the hill that separated the cottage from the Montgomery property. Her knees throbbed with each step and her head still ached. Another few days of rest might have been in order, but the thought of so much idle time filled her with dread. The last thing she wanted was time alone to think about the past. It was hard enough to keep the memories at bay when she was busy.

"Aren't you supposed to be sleeping?" Shane stepped out onto the porch, watching Raven as she approached.

She tried to straighten her spine and look less tired than she felt. "No. I'm supposed to be working. I was supposed to start Monday, remember?"

"And you got run over by a car. Remember?"

"The car barely touched me."

"Go home, Raven. You can't do Abby any good feeling like you do." The words were sharper than Shane had intended, and he wasn't surprised when Raven raised her chin stubbornly.

"We agreed that I'd meet with you when I was feeling better. I'm feeling better."

"Better wouldn't take much. I want *healthy.*" What was with this woman? Did she ever rest? The first time he'd seen her, he'd thought her a flower child with a go-with-the-flow nature. Now Shane realized the soft, flowing clothes and wild hair hid a will of steel and a spirit driven by some hurt he couldn't even begin to fathom. "Take a few more days. Come back when you feel a hundred percent."

She opened her mouth to argue, then stopped and shrugged. "Fine. I'll come back on Monday."

As she turned, Shane's eyes were drawn to her narrow shoulders. She was too thin, her body fragile beneath the bright fabric of her dress. Would she rest when she got home? He doubted it. More likely she'd clean, or cook or do some other task. Better to have her here where he could be sure she didn't overdo it.

"You're here now. Why not come in for a while? I called the home health-care agency Abby's doctor recommended. We can make up a schedule, decide when you're going to work and when I'll need one of their people to fill in."

"All right."

"Let's go into my office. Abby's with one of the agency's caregivers."

"Things are working out?"

"As well as can be expected." Shane led the way into the office and gestured to the couch, wincing in sympathy as Raven lowered herself onto the cushion. "Those knees look painful."

"Not too bad." She arranged the skirt of her dress to cover the raw, bruised flesh.

Despite her appearance, she was all business. Shane wondered what he should do with her. He couldn't send her home, not when it was so obvious she wanted to stay. He couldn't let her work, either. Ben had called twice to remind Shane that his sister wasn't up to anything more strenuous than sleep.

He glanced around the office, saw the box of doughnuts he'd brought in for a snack. He'd feed her, then give her the schedule. "Here, have a doughnut."

"No thanks. Do you keep a medical file for Abby? If

you do, I'd like to look at it before we work out the schedule."

"In the file cabinet. Eat this while I get it." He took a glazed doughnut from the box, put it on a napkin and held it out to her.

"I'm not hungry."

"You ate breakfast already?"

"I don't usually eat breakfast."

"Now's as good a time as any to start."

She wrinkled her nose and frowned, but took the doughnut. "I'm really not hungry."

"Humor me."

"Do you always get your way?"

"Only when it matters."

"And my eating this doughnut matters?"

"Ben won't thank me if he returns and finds his sister fading away to nothing."

"I'm not Ben's responsibility. Or yours."

"You have a point. So let's compromise. You eat that doughnut. I'll eat the rest of them."

"How is that a compromise?"

"I was going to try and get you to eat two."

Raven smiled at that and shook her head, dark curls brushing against her cheek. "Do you ever give up?"

Shane wondered if her hair was as soft as it looked. Wondered what Raven would think if he reached out and checked for himself. "Sometimes. But only when I'm wrong."

"Which is rare?"

"I'd say yes, but the entire town knows differently."

Raven's laughter spilled into the room, warm and inviting, and Shane felt something inside him unbalance.

He knew he was in trouble.

"And what does Abby think? Does she think you're ever wrong?"

"Think? She *knows* it. I'm pretty sure she's got written records of every mistake I've made."

"And she loves you anyway."

"That's the thing about Aunt Abby—she doesn't hold things against people. She's a strong woman. A good one. But she understands other people's weaknesses."

"I can see that in her. The strength and the compassion."

"She's the one who taught me a person could be both of those things." Shane took a bite of his doughnut and smiled as Raven ate more of hers.

"What about your parents?"

"Mom died when I was too young to remember her. Dad was gruff, to put it mildly. Abby's the only real parent I've ever had. She took me in when Dad died."

"And that's why you're so loyal to her?"

"It's more than loyalty. It's love. One of the other things Abby taught me. That and faith."

"She brought you to church?"

"She dragged me kicking and screaming. Actually, she got Nora's sons to drag me."

"It must have been nice to have someone care so much." The words slipped out before Raven could stop them.

"Yeah. It was. How about you? Did you have someone like Abby in your life?"

"My mother...tried." Not really. She'd been too immersed in her addictions to care much about her children. Only when she was sober did she love them, and then to a claustrophobic extent.

"She brought you to church?"

Raven laughed at the thought, the sound harsh and humorless even to *her* ears. "She brought me to bars.

Ben brought me to church. It was only two blocks away and we'd walk there for Vacation Bible School in the summer. I became a Christian when I was eight. It's been the only steady thing in my life since then."

"What—?"

"Maybe I could look at Abby's file now."

Shane took the hint, though Raven could see the curiosity in his eyes. "Sure. Eat your doughnut. I'll get it."

Raven eyed the sweet confection, popped a piece into her mouth and chewed. Her stomach lurched, more in welcome than in protest. Had she eaten dinner last night? Raven couldn't remember.

"Want another one?"

Raven licked sticky glaze from her fingers and shook her head. "No. One is enough."

"Here you go. The file."

The folder was thick with paperwork and neatly closed with rubber bands. "Thanks."

She expected Shane to back up. Instead he leaned down, ran a finger along the skin beside her mouth. "You've got sugar here."

Raven caught her breath and tried to still the wild beating of her heart. "Sugar?"

"From the doughnut."

"Oh. Thanks." She raised her hand to brush away what remained. Then she opened the folder, trying desperately to ignore Shane and the feelings he evoked in her.

It was difficult with him standing in front of her, his arms crossed against his chest, his dark hair slightly mussed.

"I'm fine here. If you have something to do…"

"Trying to get rid of me, Raven?"

"No. I just don't want to keep you from your work."

"You won't. I got my manuscript out on time. You know what that means, right?"

"You celebrate?"

Shane laughed. "No. I get to work on another one. Go ahead and read the file."

At first knowing Shane was in the room made it difficult for Raven to concentrate. She felt tense and uneasy, worried about the warm, easy connection she seemed to have with him. Soon, though, the quiet tap of fingers on keys eased her mind, soothing her with its gentle rhythm as she skimmed the first few pages of the folder.

She thought she'd get up, grab a pen and paper, and take notes, but the effort seemed too much and instead she read on, her eyes blurring as a week of sleepless nights caught up with her. Finally she drifted into sleep.

She stepped from the bedroom, knowing she shouldn't. Knowing where she was headed. Wanting to stop herself, but not able to. In the background Jonas was screaming his threats, his words mixing with the pounding of Raven's heart. She hurried just a little, her mind shouting to slow down, to watch her step. But she wanted out. Wanted to be gone from what she'd known for too long was going bad.

The hall stretched on and on as she rushed through it, the floor sloping and trembling beneath her feet. The stairs were there, steeper, the floor farther away. And beyond her reach was the front door...beckoning.

She raced on, felt the first step beneath her foot. Felt something shift beneath her heel. And then Jonas was there, standing at the bottom of the stairs, his face emaciated by disease, his dark eyes hollow and lifeless. Raven tried to back up, to force her feet back up the stairs, but he reached for her, his arm long and skeletal, his fingers snagging the sweatshirt she wore.

And she was falling, tumbling forward, screaming…

Raven cried out in her sleep, flailing wildly, her arm knocking the folder Shane had placed on the end table to the floor. He jumped up, lunging toward her before her frantic twisting could throw her off the couch.

With one hand on her shoulder, the other against her cheek, Shane tried to pull her from her dream. "Raven? You're dreaming. Wake up."

She screamed and sat up, her face so white Shane thought she might slide back into unconsciousness. For a moment her eyes were blank, unfocused, eerily empty. Then she blinked and fear replaced the emptiness.

"What happened? What's going on?"

"You were dreaming."

"I was?" She lifted a shaky hand to her face. "I didn't mean to fall asleep."

"You needed to sleep. You're exhausted."

"I'm sorry. I guess you were right. I should have stayed home today. I'll go now."

"Stay put. You're in no shape to go anywhere."

"I'm fine."

"That's what you always say, and most of the time it isn't true. Like right now. You're whiter than the paper I print my manuscripts on."

"I'm naturally fair."

"There's a difference between fair and dead-white. So sit still for a minute and let me get you some water."

"I can—"

"Yeah, we've been through this already. You can take

care of yourself. This time you don't have to. So sit still and let me take care of you for a minute."

Shane stalked across the room, angry for reasons he couldn't name. Mostly, he figured, it was Raven's disregard for her own well-being that had him up in arms. She didn't eat. Didn't sleep. Barely rested. The urge to turn around and tell her how foolish she was being almost overwhelmed him, but Shane had learned self-control from the best. Abby knew the value of being slow to speech.

So did Shane.

He took his time pouring ice water into a glass. Obviously Raven had secrets. Secrets she had no intention of sharing. Shane figured he should just leave her to them and let her work things out herself. But could he? As he stepped from the kitchen and saw her sitting on the couch, her brow furrowed, her eyes sad, he wondered if he even wanted to.

Raven felt dizzy, disoriented. The dream always did that to her. Worse, her heart was galloping in her chest, beating too hard. She wanted to lie back down, rest her eyes, let herself drift away from the pain that screamed inside her. But Shane was walking toward her, a glass of water in one hand and a cloth in the other, so instead she tried to smile.

"Are we gallant knight and damsel in distress today?"

He didn't respond. His face was hard, his expression grim, the frustration and anger she saw in his eyes something she'd seen often in Jonas. She turned away from it, bending to pick up the file folder that had fallen on the floor.

"Leave it." The words were a quiet command, and Raven met Shane's eyes once again.

"I don't take orders."

"You don't take anything, but this time I have to insist. You've barely got enough blood in your head to keep you upright. Lean down like that and you might pass out on your way back up."

He had a point. Raven eased back up and leaned back against the cushions as a wave of dizziness swept over her. She floated for seconds half-conscious, then felt Shane's hand on her arm, anchoring her.

"You need to take better of yourself." His voice was a growl, but Shane's hand was gentle against her arm, skimming over the cool flesh there, as he urged her to lie down.

"I do take care of myself."

"Yeah? So when was the last time you ate a meal? When was the last time you had a good night's sleep?"

She wouldn't lie, so she didn't answer.

"That's what I thought."

"There are plenty of people who work hard. Who eat when they have time. There's nothing wrong with that."

"Nothing wrong with it if the person enjoys what she's doing. If she takes time to renew herself when she needs it. Seems to me, you don't do either."

"You don't know me well enough to make that judgment."

"Maybe not, but I know what I see. I see this—" He ran a finger beneath Raven's eye. "And this—" Ran it down her cheek. "Too much color in the one, not enough in the other. You're running yourself ragged, and what I want to know is why."

"I'm a nurse. It goes with the territory."

"I don't think so. Even the most dedicated professional can take time for herself if she wants. You don't. There must be a reason."

"Not one I want to talk about."

Silence stretched between them. Then Shane sighed. "Drink your water, it'll put some color back in your cheeks."

He started to walk away, and Raven knew she didn't want to be left alone. Not with the grief and horror of the dream still fresh in her mind.

"Have you ever lost someone you loved?"

Shane stopped, turned back. "Loved? My father, I suppose. Though we didn't have much of a relationship."

"I have. It's a hard thing to get over."

"You must have loved your husband a lot."

"No. Not Jonas. Maybe when we first married, but later, things went bad."

"Then who?"

"Micah. My son."

A son? He'd imagined a lot of things about Raven; none of them had to do with her having children.

"You had a son?"

"Just for a few hours. He was born too early."

"I'm sorry."

Raven shrugged, but Shane knew it cost her to pretend indifference.

"It was a long time ago."

"Before your husband died?"

"Yes. Micah died a month before Jonas's illness was diagnosed." She sat up, pulling her legs up to her chest and resting her chin on her knees. She looked young and vulnerable, and Shane wanted to take her in his arms and protect her from all the things that tormented her. He listened instead, watching as Raven stared out the window and continued to speak.

"I didn't go home after I was released from the hospital. Didn't see my husband for five weeks. Then he called me. Said he had an inoperable brain tumor and he wanted to make amends—to ask forgiveness for what had gone wrong in our relationship. I went home to care for him."

"That was a selfless thing to do."

"No. It wasn't. I wanted to die after I lost Micah. Caring for Jonas gave me something to do. Someone to be besides the woman who lost her child—" Her voice broke and she raised a shaky hand to brush hair from her cheek.

"So you were the nurse."

"It was better than the alternative."

"How long did you nurse your husband?"

"Almost two years. He died three years ago. In the winter."

She shivered, as if reliving the day, and Shane grabbed the quilt from the back of the couch and draped it around her shoulders. "You okay?"

"Like I said, it was a long time ago."

Yet she still dreamed of it. Shane didn't point that out. There was something else, some other part of the story that she wasn't sharing, and he wanted to know what it was. Now wasn't the time to push for answers, though, not with Raven's eyes challenging Shane to question her story, to give her reason to run again. He brushed curls from her cheek, tucked them behind her ear.

"Drink your water."

She sipped, then took a deeper swallow, color blooming on her cheeks and tingeing them with rose.

"I read some of Abby's file. She's on several medications."

So, it was back to business. Shane could deal with that. At least for now. "That's right. I have a chart with doses and times."

"Good. We'll put that on a white-board and hang it on the refrigerator. Med, dose, time in permanent marker. Whoever administers the medication can sign for the day and hour."

"Sounds good."

"It's effective. Protects against overdosing or missing meds altogether." She leaned forward, grabbed the folder from the ground and stood. "Do you mind if I bring this home, go over it there?"

"Go ahead."

"I'll be back tomorrow."

Shane didn't bother arguing. "Do you want a ride home?"

"I'll walk. It's such a beautiful day. Abby should be outside. I'm sure she'd enjoy a walk."

Was that how Raven dealt with her grief, by pouring all her energy into someone else? "I'll take her out. Maybe we'll come for a visit later. I'm sure she'd like to see you."

"I'll be home. Trying to hang laundry without dragging it in the dirt."

"I've got a dryer."

"I appreciate the offer, but this is a matter of pride now. I can't let the blasted line beat me." Real humor gleamed in Raven's eyes, and Shane caught a glimpse of the woman she might have been before she'd lost her son.

And her husband.

Though it appeared Raven didn't regret his death nearly as much. That seemed at odds with what Shane had seen. Raven was the kind of person that bled a little with each death, each lost soul, each bad ending. So what had happened between her and Jonas to make her speak of his death so emotionlessly?

Shane thought about it as he walked Raven outside. Thought more about it as he watched her walk away. Her husband must have wounded her deeply for Raven to have turned her back on him.

And in the end, she hadn't completely turned away. She'd nursed him through his illness, staying with him despite her need to escape the relationship. Regardless of what she'd said, Raven's actions had been selfless. And that, in Shane's opinion, was true love. A love that gave even when it received nothing in return. A love that continued even when the feeling was gone, layered by resentment and swept away on waves of regret.

A love Shane wouldn't mind experiencing. A love he wouldn't mind giving.

The thought made him pause, his hand on the office door. *Love.* The emotion was something he hadn't had much experience with. He'd dated plenty during high school and college, but had never felt more than affection for any woman. Post-college days had been full of writing, his relationships brief—a few dinners, movies, maybe the theater.

He'd been content with the arrangement.

Was he still? Shane wasn't sure, but he had a feeling that things were changing, and changing fast. Whether he liked it or not.

Chapter Eleven

Raven didn't go straight home. Maybe she should have, but she wanted to walk off some of her tension and force the nightmare to the back of her mind. In the cottage, surrounded by four walls and loneliness, that would be difficult. But outside, with grass rustling beneath her feet and birds flitting from tree to tree, she could focus on the glorious creation around her and keep her mind off other things.

Like Micah. Like Jonas. And like Shane…

Raven could admit it to herself. Being around Shane made her feel more alive than she had in a long time. She wasn't sure she liked the feeling. Living meant feeling pain, disappointment and unhappiness. Those were things she'd left behind after Jonas's death. Things she figured she could spend the rest of her life doing without. It wasn't that she didn't want to enjoy what God gave her, or that she didn't cherish the hours and minutes of her days. But those hours, those minutes, were gifts she gave to other people. Gladly. Without regret. She wanted nothing in return, accepted nothing in return.

Shane wanted to give. Raven could see it in his eyes, hear it in his voice. His passion for life, for the good and bad of it, was clear in his writing. He wouldn't be afraid to dream of happily-ever-afters, even if he'd never had one of his own.

But Raven was afraid—afraid that another bad ending would be more than she could bear.

"Too beautiful a day for frowning."

Raven whirled toward the voice, then smiled as she caught sight of Sam Riley.

"You're right. How are you, Mr. Riley?"

"Sam. And I'm doing fine, but you seem a bit peaked. Heard what happened."

"Happened?"

"The car. Some kid joyriding, I hear."

"That's what Officer Marshal said. I haven't heard anything different yet."

"Yet?" Sam fell into step beside Raven, linked an arm through hers and began to walk. "Now, what else could it be? Seems to me, kids have been pulling pranks like that for years. Won't change, no matter how much the law might want it to."

"I'm sure that's all it was. Officer Marshal just wanted to be sure it was an accident."

"I may be old but I've still got a brain in my head. If it wasn't an accident, then someone tried to kill you or Abby."

Spoken aloud the suspicion sounded absurd. "Like I said. The police are just checking out every angle."

"What angle?"

"Officer Marshal said someone might have motive for hurting Abby."

"Not someone. If Marshal's accusing, he's talking about Shane."

"The police just need to—"

"Not the police. Marshal. He and Shane have been feuding since high school. Some fight over a girl, I think. Can't remember all the details."

"That was a long time ago. I doubt there are still hard feelings."

Sam stopped short and peered down into Raven's face. Then he shook his head. "Don't kid yourself. People around here have long memories."

"Like with Thea Trebain?"

"Yeah. Just like that. Let's walk some more."

For a moment Raven considered refusing. There'd been something in Sam's tone that set alarms off in her mind. Then he raised an eyebrow, his features relaxing into a smile.

"Don't worry, I won't bite."

"You seem upset that I mentioned Thea."

"Not upset, just curious. Wondering what a young gal like you is doing worrying about ancient history."

"Not worrying. Wondering. You've got to admit it's an intriguing tale."

"Now, see, that's just it. It's not a *tale* at all. When you say Thea's story is an intriguing tale, you forget the humanity in it. That people mourned her. Grieved for her."

"And you were one of them."

Sam turned away, his shoulders sagging beneath the weight of his emotion. "We were friends. I would have been more, but she never wanted me. Always loved someone else."

"I'm sorry."

"Don't be." He turned, the smile back on his face. "I

married Anna instead. We had a real love, the kind built on friendship and shared dreams. I knew long before Thea disappeared that we wouldn't have been happy together. My feelings were a childish crush. Nothing more. That doesn't mean I want people to take Thea's disappearance lightly."

"I don't. I'm sorry if you felt that way."

"Don't worry about it. I'm a grumpy old man—just like my granddaughter is always saying. Come on. Gotta get back to the house before Tori finds out I'm gone."

"You're not supposed to leave the house?"

"Doctor appointment later on. Missed the last one and Tori's on the warpath."

"Are you ill?"

"Nah. A little trouble with the blood pressure that's all. I take my medication, I'm fine."

"Can I ask you something, Sam? Something about Thea?"

"Guess that depends on what it is."

"What do you think happened? Really."

"Don't think. *Know.* She's dead. Has been since the day she disappeared."

"But how can you know that?"

"Thea was a lot of things—hardheaded, stubborn, too pretty for her own good. But she wasn't a coward. No way she'd run from her problems."

"Problems?"

"You mean no one's told you?"

"Told me what?"

"Thea was having an affair. Or so the story goes."

"So it isn't a fact?"

"Didn't say that, did I? A story always has a grain of truth. Thea was having an affair. Some say with a married man. Some say with an out-of-towner. Some say he was black. Some say he was white."

"What do you think? You were her friend."

"I think there was only one man Thea ever loved. If she had an affair, it was with him."

"Who?"

"Daniel Meade."

"Abby's brother? He was married."

"Married with a son and three daughters. Adam was maybe seventeen or eighteen at the time. The girls, a few years younger."

"Did they know about the affair?"

"Who knows? Thea'd been away for years. Left town after Daniel married and didn't return until her mother fell ill. Must have been fifteen or sixteen years later. Most people 'round here had finally stopped talking about the relationship the two had had before Daniel married. When Thea came back, rumors started flying again. I'd be surprised if Daniel's kids didn't hear something of it. But did they think he'd have an affair with her? That I can't say."

"How about his wife? Did she know?"

"If she did, I doubt she cared. Allison was a cold woman. Still is."

"So why marry her?"

"That's something only Daniel could say. Though I'd venture a guess his father had something to do with it." Sam stopped speaking and raised an eyebrow. "You're awfully curious about something that happened before you were born."

"I've heard Thea mentioned several times. I guess I just wondered what happened to her."

"You and everyone else. Wish I had a real answer, but I don't."

"Thanks for sharing what you do know."

"No problem. Hey, how's the puppy working out?"

"Merry's great. Come to the house if you want—you can visit."

"Nope. Tori'll have my head if I miss my appointment again. Got to go." He saluted and turned away.

Raven watched him go, wondering about the things he'd told her. How accurate were they, colored as they were by Sam's skewed perspective? Daniel and Thea had both been his friends. Could he see their human frailties through the love he so obviously had for them?

Raven didn't know and wasn't sure she should care. Yet the story of Thea Trebain haunted her. Abby had been deeply affected by her friend's disappearance. Did she know something, something that perhaps her best friend and her brother had revealed to her? A secret meant to be kept, but now being revealed? And would that revelation ease Abby's mind, or stir up old demons?

Raven shook her head at the thought, pushed open the cottage door—and stepped into chaos. Fabric trailed along the floor. The couch was flipped over, the cushions slit and leaking stuffing. Framed pictures lay in beds of shattered glass. Shredded books were scattered like confetti around the room. A creak broke the silence. The sound soft, subtle and out of place. Raven froze. Her breath was shallow and quiet, her ears straining to hear above the sound of her own heartbeat.

Was that the quiet padding of feet she heard? And where was Merry? She'd yet to make an appearance— no whining, barking or paws scratching against the kitchen floor to say she was all right. Raven swallowed down her fear and took a step into the room. A loud crash sent her jumping back.

She didn't wait to hear more. She raced out the door and across the yard, her heart pounding so hard she thought it might burst from her chest. The driveway seemed too long; the road stretched endlessly. Raven didn't look back, didn't dare turn to see if someone was coming after her. She just raced back the way she'd come, back toward the Montgomerys. Back to safety. Back to Shane.

A hard knock on the door jerked Shane from his work, dragging him back from his mystical fictional world into reality. He wasn't sure he wanted to go. The knock sounded again, and he knew he'd lost the flow of the story. Irritated, he shoved away from the desk and stalked to the door, swinging it open with enough force to send it crashing into the wall.

"What! I'm trying to work…" The words died as he caught sight of Raven. Her face was white, her eyes frantic.

Shane tugged her inside the office, ran his hands along the cold flesh of her arms. "What's wrong? What happened?"

"Someone's at the cottage. Trashed it." She panted the words out, her hands trembling as she pressed them against her stomach.

"Are you hurt? Did he hurt you?" The thought made Shane go cold with fear and rage.

"No. I didn't actually *see* anyone. Just a lot of damage."

"Sit down. I'll call the police."

For once she didn't argue, didn't try to maintain control. She just sat silent and pale as Shane made the call.

"They'll be here in a minute."

"I need to go back."

"The dispatcher told me we should wait here."

"Merry's missing. What if…?" Her voice broke and her eyes filled, though no tears fell.

"Who'd hurt a puppy?"

"Someone who would break into a house and trash it."

She had a point, but Shane didn't say so. "Don't worry. She probably ran and hid."

Raven didn't think so. The puppy was too friendly for her own good. If the intruder had approached her with a baseball bat in one hand and a shotgun in the other, Merry would have sat on her little rump, tail wagging and tongue lolling.

Where were the police? The wait seemed endless, though it was less than ten minutes after Shane's call that Raven heard the first siren. Another followed seconds later.

"I'll go out and meet them." Shane started toward the door, and Raven stood and hurried after him.

"I'll go with you."

By the time they made it down the stairs and around the side of the house, the first cruiser was pulling up. An officer stepped out, his hat shadowing his face. Raven recognized him anyway, the height and the breadth of his shoulders clearly marking him as Jake Reed.

"Hear you've got some trouble."

Raven nodded, stepped forward and felt the weight of Shane's hand rest on her shoulder. It felt good, welcome, and for once she didn't pull away, didn't force herself to deny the comfort and support he offered. He stayed beside her as Jake approached.

"Why don't you tell me what you saw at the cottage. I've got men there now, checking things out. I'll get the facts from you, then join them."

Raven did as she was asked, speaking in the quiet monotone of a person in shock. She recognized this, but told herself she was fine. Just as she always had been, as she always would be.

After a few questions, Jake seemed satisfied and closed the notebook he'd been writing in. "All right. We'll check things out. When we're done, I'll come get you and bring you home. We'll do a walk-through. See if anything's missing."

There was no question in his voice, just a simple statement of the way things would be. It needed no response, and Raven gave none.

"What's going on, dear? Is that an ambulance?" Abby stepped outside, a young Asian woman beside her.

"A police car, Aunt Abby. There's been a break-in at the cottage."

"Oh, no. Is everyone okay?"

"Raven's fine."

"What about Nora and the boys? Her husband's out of town, you know."

Raven wondered what Shane would say to that. Would he try to argue with his aunt's faulty memory? Would he play along?

He did neither. "I'm sure they're all fine. You were a great neighbor to them." He paused, squeezed Raven's shoulder. "This is Raven, Aunt Abby. She lives in the cottage now."

"Hello, dear." Abby squinted, her gaze focusing on Raven as if seeing her for the first time. "I'm sorry to hear you've had trouble. Would you like a cup of tea?"

"That would be nice. Thanks."

They walked into the kitchen together, the aide leading Abby to a chair and helping her sit. Raven moved to the stove and the teakettle, hoping to keep her hands busy and her mind off what was happening at the cottage.

"Anyone else want a cup?" she asked.

"Let me do that." Shane shifted close to Raven, edging into her space so that his arm brushed hers as he grabbed the teakettle from her hand, filled it and set it to boil. "You okay?"

"I'm fine. Just anxious to know what's going on."

"It shouldn't take Jake long to get back."

His hand came to rest on her neck, kneading tense muscles there and offering comfort she didn't want to need but seemed helpless to deny. She leaned against him, allowing herself a moment of comfort. Then, realizing what she was doing, how dangerous it could be, she stepped back, grabbing teacups from the cupboard.

"Did you want tea, Shane?"

"I'm thinking something stronger might be in order."

"Stronger?"

"Sure." He reached into the refrigerator and pulled out two soda bottles. "This stuff packs a wallop. I think they put in extra caffeine."

"Maybe I should give it a try. I could use a pick-me-up. But first, let's get Abby her tea."

"I can do that." The aide stepped forward as the sound of an approaching car engine drifted through the open window.

Jake was already coming up the porch steps as Raven and Shane stepped back outside. "No one's in the house. We've dusted for prints. We'll get yours, as well as those of the people who've visited you recently. Don't know if we'll come up with anything, but it's worth a try. Ready to go?"

"Yes." Not really. She'd rather stay put. Go back into

Shane and Abby's warm kitchen, drink her soda and forget the reality of what had happened.

"Good. Let's go. Oh yeah, I almost forgot. I found something of yours. Thought you might want to have it back." He opened the back of the cruiser, reached in and pulled Merry out. "She's scared, but seems fine otherwise."

"Merry!" Raven grabbed the puppy, pulled her close and kissed her head. "Thank goodness. I was so worried. Where'd you find her?"

"Cowering in the bathroom."

"Poor thing. Are you okay?"

Shane listened to Raven coo and cosset the ugly little pup. She seemed smitten, completely oblivious to the fact that her dog looked like nothing so much as a giant rat.

"She isn't ugly."

Raven's comment startled Shane from his thoughts and he met her gaze, doing his best to look innocent and benign. "I never said she was."

"No. But you're thinking it. I can see it in your eyes."

"My eyes—"

"Let's save your defense for another time, Shane," said Jake. "Right now I want to get Raven home."

The humor Shane had seen dancing at the corner of Raven's mouth disappeared. She seemed to shrink back, as if cowering from some unspoken fear. Then, as quickly as it had come, the look of fear was gone and she straightened her spine and stepped forward. "I'll have to call Nora when we get to the cottage. She'll need to know what happened."

"I called her a few minutes ago. She's on her way."

"I feel terrible about this. I hope there isn't too much damage."

"There isn't. And even if there was, it wouldn't be your fault. Seems to me what happened would have happened whether you were in the house or not."

Jake's words were meant to reassure, but Shane could see that Raven didn't believe them. He wasn't sure he did, either.

He stepped past Jake and leaned in close to Raven. "Why don't I come with you? I can help you clean up the mess."

For a moment he thought she'd agree, but she shook her head, her desire for independence apparently stronger than her need for support and help.

"I appreciate the offer, Shane, but Abby needs you."

"She's got her aide."

"Thanks. But I'll be okay."

Shane whispered close to her ear. "We can't always go it alone. God didn't design us that way."

She blinked, her discomfort at his comment obvious. She might have spoken, perhaps argued, but Jake stepped behind Shane and slapped a heavy hand against his shoulder, the gesture too rough to be friendly.

"She said she's fine."

Shane whirled, ready to let loose the anger and frustration he felt. Then Raven's hand slipped into his, tugging him back and holding him still. He glanced down, saw the almost pleading expression in her eyes, and knew he'd tread carefully with Jake, if only to ease Raven's anxiety.

"All right. Call if you need something, Raven."

"I will."

But they both knew she wouldn't. And Shane wondered as he watched Jake's car retreating down the driveway, why he cared so much.

Chapter Twelve

Raven knew things were bad at the cottage and had expected the worst. Still, she gasped as she stepped across the threshold and got a better look at the damage. To say the house was a mess was like saying a hurricane was a spring storm. Papers were strewn across the floor, books ripped from their bindings, pictures slashed and torn. It seemed an act of senseless violence, the purpose beyond anything Raven could imagine.

They walked from room to room, lifting items, checking closets, drawers, Raven's jewelry box...her heart thudded as she lifted the small teak-wood box from the floor. The items it contained were scattered across the dresser and floor, and she bent to pick them up, cataloging each in her mind, searching for the only one that meant anything to her.

It wasn't there.

She searched the floor, found her wedding band, the diamond studs Jonas had given her for their first wedding anniversary, the bracelet she'd gotten from a patient. But no silver locket. She felt dizzy with the knowledge, her body swaying.

"You okay?" Jake put a hand on her arm, holding her steady.

"Fine." But she wasn't. Not if the locket was missing.

"We looking for anything in particular?"

"A silver locket. Large. On a long chain. Victorian era."

"Valuable?"

"It's worth the price of the silver, anyway." And it was priceless to Raven.

Jake pulled a penlight from his pocket and shone it under the dresser. There was nothing there. Not even dust. He did the same to the area under the bed and beneath the armoire. Then he helped Raven lift piles of clothes that had been pulled from the drawers and closet.

With each item moved, each crevice searched with no sign of the locket, the storm inside Raven grew, until she didn't know how she'd contain it.

"You sure you're okay? You're trembling."

A sweater landed on Raven's shoulders and she pulled it tight around herself. "Thanks. I'm freezing."

"You're in shock."

"I don't understand why someone would do this. And why take the locket and not the earrings? They're worth much more."

"Wish I had some answers for you, but until we find the person responsible, we can't know the motive. And even after we find that person, we might not have an answer."

Raven nodded but didn't speak. She couldn't, not with the lump in her throat.

"So far we've got a missing locket." Jake made a note in his notebook. "Anything else?"

"No. I don't think so."

They moved into the kitchen and Raven winced. Flour and sugar coated the floor in a thick layer. Broken dishes, cups and containers littered the counter and table. Everywhere she looked, destruction. Was anything else missing? She ran a hand through her hair, trying to force her mind from the missing locket and back to the task at hand. "The cookie tin's missing."

Jake raised an eyebrow. "Cookie tin?"

"Used as a keepsake box. There were a few pieces of jewelry in it. Thea's diary is missing, too. My laptop was sitting on the table. It's gone. My Bible's gone, too."

Several other items were missing and Raven listed them. "That's it, I think."

"Odd mix of items."

It was. Raven wasn't sure what that meant, or if it meant anything at all. All she knew was that she wanted to go through the cottage again, recheck every room and search under the piles of debris, in the hope that the locket was there.

"Oh my, this is terrible." Nora walked into the room, her face lined with worry. "Who would do such a thing?"

"I don't know, Ms. Freedman, but I plan to find out. You want to walk through, see if any of the original furniture and paintings are missing?"

It didn't take long for Nora to make a tour of the house. She returned minutes later. "Nothing's missing as far as I can see."

"Thea's diary and keepsake box were taken. I'm so sorry, I'm sure her family will be disappointed."

"They'll understand. I'm not sure they were that interested, anyway. Most of them didn't even know Thea."

"Still—"

"Now, don't waste time worrying. Things'll work out. Was anything of yours taken?"

"A few things. Jake has the list."

He stepped forward. "Looks like we've done all we can for now. I'll have people keep an eye out at local pawnshops, see if any of the items show up."

Raven winced as she imagined her locket being bought by a stranger, the photo ripped out and thrown away.

"You okay, doll? You've gone pale."

Nora's concern was obvious, and Raven tried to smile a reassurance.

"I'm fine. Is there anything else I need to do before I start cleaning up, Jake?"

"The lock will need to be replaced. Looks like someone jimmied it open. Dead bolt's still good. Make sure you use it."

"I will."

He nodded and stepped outside.

"Guess we'd better get started on this mess." Nora grabbed a broom and began sweeping up glass and flour.

"I'll do that, Nora. It won't take me long to get this cleaned up."

"I don't mind. Do you have some trash bags?"

Raven didn't argue further—just grabbed trash bags from a drawer and set to work, eager to get busy and force her mind away from the missing locket.

Nora kept up a steady stream of conversation as they tidied, and Raven joined in as best she could, her mind fumbling for answers to the simplest questions, until Nora paused, her hand on a pile of torn paper, and looked at her.

"You're quiet."

"I'm sorry. I'm not in the mood for conversation."

"I understand. My way of dealing is to talk. When my husband passed away, I spent two full days talking about nothing." She smiled, the expression bittersweet. "Harold used to call me Chatter. 'Course, he was a quiet one—never much to say unless it was really important."

"He must have been a wonderful man."

"He was. Actually, all the Freedmans were good people. Though I have to say, my Harold was the best of the bunch."

"Did you grow up together?"

"Went to the same high school. Got married as soon as we graduated. Moved to this cottage for a while, then across town when the boys got older. Not enough room in this place for three teenage boys."

"I imagine not. Did Thea have many siblings?"

Nora shot a look in Raven's direction, but answered the question. "She was an only child."

"Is that why your husband took care of the cottage for Thea?"

"Yes. He was a few years younger than Thea, but they were close. Like brother and sister. When she disappeared, we took care of the property, made sure the taxes were paid—all the things that needed to be done to keep the cottage habitable in case Thea returned. Eventually the family decided Harold should have the property."

"That makes sense."

"Harold would have preferred to return the property to Thea, but she never came home."

Raven wanted to ask more, but Nora didn't give her a chance. "Looks like we've got things cleaned up. Insurance should cover the damage. I'll call in the claim and give you a ring later this week. I'd better head home now, though. The grandkids are coming by tonight."

"Thanks for helping with the cleanup. I'm so sorry this happened."

"You've got no fault in this, so there's no need to apologize." She smiled and stepped out onto the porch. "Do like Jake said and keep the doors bolted."

"I will."

Raven watched Nora get into her car and drive away, then closed and locked the door. The silence of the house wasn't as comforting as she wanted it to be, so she picked Merry up and hugged her close as she made her way back through the living room and into the bedroom. Maybe, just maybe, they'd missed the locket and it was still hidden somewhere in the house.

It was a long shot, probably an impossibility, but Raven couldn't rest until she checked one last time.

"Montgomery!"

Shane didn't need to glance up from the lawn mower he was trying to start to know who'd called his name. He looked up anyway, despite the childish urge to ignore the man.

"Jake."

"Got a minute?"

"Depends. If you're here to lecture me on Ben's sister, then no. If it's something else, maybe."

"Guess we're both in luck. I'll meet you on the porch."

Shane took his time, dusting his hands off on the faded jeans he wore, ramming the baseball cap a little tighter onto his head. When he finally moved toward the porch it was with the leisurely steps of someone who had all the time in the world. Which, he imagined, as he caught sight of Jake's dark blue eyes, irritated his guest.

"What can I do for you, Jake?"

"Move a little faster, for one."

Shane didn't bother hiding his grin as he stepped onto the porch. "Sorry."

"Sure you are."

They eyed each other in silence for a moment. Then Jake held out a hand. "We got started on the wrong foot. I wanted to apologize."

In the face of Shane's childish behavior, the gesture and words were burning coals being poured, with purpose, onto his head.

"Don't pull your punches, do you."

Reed had the nerve to smile, his teeth flashing in an expression that was more triumphant than friendly. "Not usually. How about you?"

"I would have done the same." He clasped the other man's hand and restrained himself from testing his strength against Jake's grip.

"Yeah, I thought we were more alike than not."

"So, what brings you here?"

"Raven Stevenson."

"Thought this wasn't about her."

"It isn't about *you* and her. It's about her. You know much about her?"

"Not a lot. Why?"

"Something's bothering her. Something more than the cottage being trashed. Couldn't put my finger on it, but it's been worrying me. I called Ben. He wants to cut his trip short, but he's afraid she'll run if he pushes too hard."

"Makes sense. Raven doesn't seem like the kind to

want to be coddled. I can see her running from too much attention."

Jake's brows arched. "I thought you said you didn't know her well."

"I'm a writer—analyzing people is what I do." Shane met the other man's doubt head-on. "I don't see what any of what you've said has to do with me."

"Maybe nothing. Maybe a lot. Depends on how much you want to stick your nose into your neighbor's business."

"Go on."

"Something's up. I don't know what yet, but I don't like the pattern. First a car almost hits Raven, now her house has been broken into and trashed."

"A burglary?"

"Made to look like one, anyway. But there were too many valuables left behind. Diamond earrings, a ring, a CD player."

"Could be the thief was in a hurry."

"Or it could be someone wants us to think that."

"Why?"

"I've been asking myself the same question. Don't have an answer yet, but I plan to get one. In the meantime, I thought you could keep your eyes and ears open—check in on Raven when you get a chance, maybe try to get her to stay with Abby a few nights. Just until we figure out what's going on."

"No problem. Anything else?"

"Yeah. Watch your back. My gut says things aren't what they seem."

"Will do. Tell Ben I'm keeping an eye on Raven until he gets back."

Jake nodded and started back to the cruiser. "See ya."

Shane paced the porch, running his hand along the rail, trying to fit the pieces of the puzzle together. Things had been calm, normal, even a little boring before Raven's arrival. Now they were anything but.

It was easy to believe she'd brought the trouble with her. Not so easy to think she'd wronged somebody enough to have such a savage revenge exacted. So what else could it be? Coincidence? Maybe—though Shane found it hard to imagine that the runaway car and the trashed house weren't connected in some way.

"Mr. Montgomery?" Becca stepped out onto the porch with Abby. Both wore lightweight slacks, cotton tops in bright colors, and smiles.

It was good to see Abby happy for a change.

"Yes?"

"Ms. Abby is craving chocolate ice cream. I thought I'd take her to get some. We'll stay in the car, if you like. Just go to the drive-through."

Shane hesitated, his worry for Abby's well-being rearing up in protest. "How long will you be gone?"

"No more than an hour. I'll bring my cell phone and pager. If there's trouble, I know how to reach you."

"You up for ice cream, Aunt Abby?"

"Pudding would be lovely." The words were muddled, but her smile didn't fade. "I need to go."

Shane was sure there was something more Abby wanted besides ice cream. Perhaps just a chance to be out without him. "Have fun, then." He kissed his aunt on the cheek, then spoke softly to Becca. "Take good care of her."

"Don't worry. She'll be fine."

Shane knew she would. He still had to force himself not to call the women back as they slid into Becca's car.

Let them go have some ice cream and enjoy the day. And while they were gone, he'd check on their neighbor, make sure Raven was holding up. Not that he expected her to do anything else. She was strong— probably stronger than Ben and Jake realized, but maybe weaker than she was willing to admit.

That, and Shane's own gut instinct, had him locking up and heading to the cottage. He walked, enjoying the warmth of the sun and the sweet, heady fragrance of the day. He wondered at his own desire to see Raven. It felt right, somehow, the deep need to see for himself that she was unharmed. Still, he mulled it over in his mind as he walked down the driveway that led to the cottage. Should he allow himself more than friendly interest? If he did, where would it lead?

He didn't know. What he did know was that Raven interested him—her quiet dignity, her faith, her servant spirit, as well as the tough exterior, so at odds with the sadness he saw in her eyes. There was a reason God had brought them together. Maybe just for Abby and maybe for something more.

Only time would tell. For now, Shane would have to trust God to lead him in the right direction, because he sure didn't know what it was. With that thought to guide him, he raised his hand and knocked on the cottage door.

Chapter Thirteen

Raven heard the rap of a fist against the front door and ignored it. She wasn't up to company. What she wanted, what she needed, was to find the locket. Merry whined at her feet as she moved across the bedroom and bent down to look under the dresser again. The locket hadn't miraculously appeared there. Nor had it appeared under the bed, the pillows or in the dresser drawers. She checked and double-checked the areas she'd searched with Jake, moving from the bedroom into the hall, and then into the living room.

"Raven? It's Shane. You okay in there?" The words drifted through the front door, accompanied by more knocking.

Raven wanted to call out and tell him she was fine, but her throat was tight with unshed tears and she was sure if she spoke, everything she felt would seep into the words. Instead she walked to the door and pulled it open, stepping back so Shane could move into the room.

"Everything all right? I've been knocking for a while."

"Everything's fine."

"You sure?" He reached to smooth a strand of hair away from her cheek, his fingers lingering, his gaze intent.

"Yes—" But her voice broke, and she turned away.

"Tell me what's wrong. Maybe I can help."

"It's nothing. Not really, it's just…my locket's missing and it meant a lot to me." A tear escaped and she scrubbed it away, impatient with herself and her emotions.

"What's it look like? I'll help you find it."

"It's turn-of-the century silver, round, on a long, thick chain. Micah's photo is inside it. The only one I have of him."

"I'm sorry." His hands cupped her shoulders and he urged her around and into his arms.

"Me, too."

"We'll find it."

"No. We won't. It's gone. Just like Micah. I should have been more careful."

"Are you talking about the locket? Or what happened to your son?"

"Both." One tear fell. Then another and another—silent, racking sobs that Raven fought but couldn't contain.

Shane's arms tightened around her. "It's okay. It'll be okay."

"No, it won't. He's gone. It's my fault. I should never have gotten pregnant. Shouldn't have stayed with Jonas once I did. But I wanted it so much. The happy family. Love. A baby."

"You can't blame yourself for what happened."

"I can. I do." Raven stepped away and forced back her tears.

"Raven—"

"I can't talk about this, Shane. I *won't* talk about it."

"Maybe you need to talk about it."

"All the talking in the world can't change what happened." She brushed her hand against her damp cheeks.

"You're right, but sometimes it helps to share our burdens."

Raven laughed, the sound harsh. "What's to share? No one can take away the pain I feel. No one can give me back what I lost. All anyone can do is feel sorry for me."

"Would that be so bad?"

"No, but it isn't something I need. What I need is to move on with my life."

Raven stepped into the kitchen and pulled a glass from the cupboard. "Want something to drink?"

"No, thanks." Shane watched Raven fill the glass with water. Her hand shook a little and her eyes were still red from tears. Obviously she *hadn't* moved on with her life. He wanted to offer words of comfort, maybe say something profound, something that would help her heal, but he was better at fiction than reality and he figured anything he said would do more harm than good.

He paced across the room. "Look, I don't know a lot about grief and healing, but I do know it isn't healthy to shove down what we feel."

"I'm not. I'm just choosing not to discuss it."

"It's the same thing, isn't it?"

"Maybe. But it's easier to move forward if I don't look back too often."

"I can understand that."

"Can you?" She slid her glass onto the counter and turned to stare out the window above the sink. "Do you have things you regret, Shane? Things that make you want to relive a moment in your life, to do just one thing differently so that an outcome can be changed?"

"Everyone has regrets."

"I know, some of us just have more than others." The sadness in her voice was unmistakable, but her eyes were dry when she turned to face him again. "When I look back at the past few years, I see one long series of mistakes and I wonder—if I could change one thing, would it make any difference? Would I still have my son?"

"That's something you can't know."

"And it's why I can't look back. There are too many what-ifs, too many moments I might have changed, but didn't." She smiled, the expression made sad by the grief in her eyes. "I need to move on, not look back. That's why I'm here. It's why I came to see Ben. He's family, and family is something I've wanted for a long time."

"Wasn't your husband your family?"

She raised an eyebrow at the question, then shrugged, as if the answer didn't matter. "My husband was self-centered and cold. Our ideas about family and marriage were different. I wanted children—the more the better. He would have been happy with none."

"Still, you loved each other. That's family, isn't it?"

"I don't know what family is. I've never really had one. I'm not sure I know what love is, either."

"Love is what happens when you care for someone else more than you care for yourself. Family is love that's reciprocated."

"A simplified definition."

"Maybe. But I'm not much for complicated emotions."

"I would have thought the opposite. Aren't writers supposed to understand the deepest human sentiments?"

"Guess that depends on who the writer is. Me, I'm

better at writing about emotions than I am at understanding them."

"Not when it comes to Abby. You're wonderful with her."

Shane recognized her attempt to change the subject and didn't fight it. "I'm just giving back to her what she gave to me."

"That doesn't make it any less wonderful. Most people take as much as they can and give little or nothing in return."

"Is that what your life has been? People taking from you and never giving back?"

Raven stiffened. "You must think I'm very cynical."

"I think you've been hurt a lot and I wonder how you've managed to stay compassionate and caring despite it."

"I'm not always compassionate and caring."

"No one is, but I think you've got more of those traits than most people."

"I'm a nurse. It's in the job description." Her words were light, her discomfort at his personal comment obvious.

Shane was tempted to say more, just to see her blush again, but knew it was better to let things lie. "I'd better get going."

He pulled the door open, stepping out into the warmth of the day, and was surprised when Raven followed, Merry scampering out close on her heels.

A light breeze ruffled Raven's hair as she walked down the porch steps, dark strands of it clinging to cheeks flushed pink with heat and tears. She looked young, too young to be a widow and a grieving mother, but grief had no boundaries. The evidence of that was clear in her eyes.

"I'm sorry about your locket. I know how much it meant to you."

"It's okay."

"No, it's not. But maybe I can make it better. I've got some friends in the antiques business. They have lots of contacts. If the locket shows up at a pawnshop or antiques store in the area, they'll hear about it."

"You don't have to—"

"I know. But I will anyway." Shane leaned in and brushed a kiss against her cheek, meaning the gesture to be a friendly one. It felt like more. Much more.

Raven must have sensed the same. Her eyes widened, though she didn't pull back.

"Shane, I don't think—"

He put a finger against her mouth, stilling the words before she could speak them. "Relax. I'm leaving. Call if you need anything."

"Thanks."

"You still up to working with Abby?"

"Of course."

"I'll see you Monday, then." With that he turned and walked away.

Raven knew it was best that he leave, but she was not sure she wanted to spend the rest of the day alone. That worried her. Until she'd come to Lakeview she'd enjoyed her solitude, never feeling lonely or ill at ease when she was by herself. Now, in just a few short days, she'd begun to crave the company of others.

No. That wasn't quite the truth. She'd begun to crave *Shane's* company. His laid-back attitude and casual manner made being near him easy. That and his genuine concern for her well-being tempted Raven to trust him.

She rubbed a hand against the warmth that seemed to linger where Shane's lips had touched her cheek. It had been years since a man had touched her, years since she'd been kissed. It would be easy to believe that was the reason she'd been so affected by the sweet caress, so warmed by his presence.

But she knew better. There'd been other men since Jonas died, men who had offered companionship, friendship, even marriage. Raven had never been tempted. She'd learned a hard lesson from her first marriage and she had no intention of repeating her mistakes.

She sighed and whistled for Merry.

"Come on, let's go inside and get you something to eat."

She opened the door and was about to step inside when Merry lunged back toward the porch steps, growling, the hair on the back of her neck standing on end. Raven jerked back, reaching for the door, ready to flee inside the house.

"Sorry to startle you and the puppy. I knocked on the front door and no one answered."

Raven heard the voice before she saw the speaker and she turned quickly as a man stepped around the corner of the cottage.

Tall, maybe fifty, with the polished air of someone use to the limelight, he looked familiar, though Raven couldn't place the face. "Can I help you?"

"I'm Adam Meade. We met at church last week." He held out his hand and smiled, the expression without warmth.

The son of the man who'd killed himself…the knowledge popped into Raven's mind, unbidden. "That's right. You're Abby's nephew."

"Right. I'm on my way to visit her and thought I'd stop by and touch base with you. Mind if I come in for a minute?"

She did. Her reluctance was instinctive, the need to keep him outside almost overwhelming. She glanced at Merry, who had stopped barking and was eyeing the newcomer warily. "I was planning to take my puppy for a walk."

It was a lie and she was sure Adam knew it. His smile didn't waver, though, and he stepped up onto the back porch.

"I really won't take much of your time. I've got a meeting after I visit Abby, so I'm on a tight schedule."

She shrugged. "Come in, then. What can I do for you, Mr. Meade?"

"Adam."

"Adam. What can I do for you?"

"Shane told me you're going to take part in Abby's care."

"That's right."

"I'm worried about my aunt. She's taken a turn for the worse lately. Living in the past more. Wandering from home. In my opinion, she should be in a facility designed to care for people with her condition."

"That's a decision the family has to make."

"But don't you think being here, being so close to her past is making her worse? Don't you think that moving her to less familiar surroundings will help draw her back to the present?"

"It's good for Abby to be near things and people she recognizes. But, as I said, that's the family's decision."

Adam's face tightened at her words, and his eyes, already cold, gleamed with an expression that made Raven shiver. When he spoke, his words were calm and smooth, but the ice beneath them was unmistakable.

"I'd hoped you'd see my point and help me get Abby the intervention she needs."

"I'm sorry, that's something I can't do."

"Can't? Or won't?"

"I'm a nurse. My job is to provide health care, support, maybe even a willing ear. What I can't provide are answers. That's something you and the rest of your family have to do."

"I'm disappointed. I don't like to waste my time."

"It isn't a waste. We got a chance to meet again. Now when Abby mentions you, I'll know who she's talking about."

Raven had meant the comment to lighten the tension. Instead Adam's expression changed, slid from cool anger to something she couldn't define.

"Like I said, I hate to waste my time. Obviously, that's what I'm doing. I need to get going. If you change your mind, call me." He slid a business card across the counter and stalked out the back door.

Raven hurried to the door and locked it behind Adam. Then she closed the kitchen window and checked the other doors and windows in the house. With the windows and doors locked against some unnamed threat, she fed Merry, grabbed paper and pen, and began making a list of what needed to be replaced.

But even as she listed items, her mind wandered back to Adam's visit—to his odd insistence that she support his effort to get Abby into an assisted living facility. What was it with the men in Abby's life? Each seemed to have his own agenda. Shane had said he'd made a promise to Abby—one he intended to keep. But was that the truth? Raven thought of Officer Marshal and his belief that Shane was motivated by more than simple affection. Raven didn't believe it.

And what of Abby's son? Mark said he loved his mother, that he wanted what was best for her, yet he wasn't willing to spend the time caring for her.

And Adam. His concern seemed feigned, his attempt to get Abby into an assisted living facility, odd. What did he have to gain by getting her out of the way? Raven blinked at the thought. Was she conjuring something sinister out of simple concern? There was no denying the runaway car or the ransacked cottage—but did they have something to do with Abby? Or was Raven the target?

She set the pen down and gazed out the kitchen window, her mind rushing from question to question, searching for answers but finding none. All she knew for sure was that something was going on—something dangerous. Maybe even deadly.

Chapter Fourteen

Raven spent the next few days driving to antiques dealers and pawnshops, searching for her locket. Though she knew the search was futile, she couldn't bring herself to give up. By Sunday she was antsy and irritable, ready for a distraction from her troubles. She rose early, well before dawn painted the sky with gold, and stepped out onto the front porch. Predawn quiet wove a spell across the countryside and Raven breathed in the cool, spring air.

She wanted to enjoy the beauty of her new home, wanted to let the silence fill her with a sense of peace and rightness. Instead she felt broken, empty, and in desperate need of something she couldn't define. She knew the reason. Despite what she'd said to Shane, she hadn't moved on with her life. She couldn't forgive or forget the mistakes she'd made. Mistakes God had allowed.

There was bitterness in the thought and an anger that Raven refused to acknowledge. Though she prayed about it often, the prayers fell flat, the words nothing more than lip service to something she wasn't sure she believed. If God had a better plan, if He was somehow making beauty out of the wreckage of her life, Raven couldn't see it.

But maybe that was the point. Maybe *that* was faith—believing even when there was nothing left to hope for.

She sighed. Too many restless nights were making her tired and melancholy. It would be good to go to work, good to focus on someone aside from herself. Tomorrow she'd be with Abby and would have little time to think about the emptiness of her life. For now she'd make do with a hot shower and a cup of mint tea.

By the time she arrived at church she felt marginally better, and smiled at a few familiar faces as she stepped into the sanctuary. She settled in a back pew, her gaze wandering along the rows of people in front of her as she waited for the service to begin. Though she told herself she wasn't looking for anyone in particular, she knew the truth. She was looking for Shane.

He wasn't there and, though Raven caught sight of Mark and Laura Montgomery, there was no sign of Abby, either. Perhaps one of them was ill. She hoped not. Abby's condition was fragile enough without added complications.

"Now, here's a sight for sore eyes. Mind if I join you?" Sam Riley slipped into the pew beside Raven, a smile lighting his dark eyes.

"How are you, Sam?"

"I'm fine. Heard *you* had some more trouble, though."

"I'm afraid so."

"Sorry to hear it. There isn't much crime in Lakeview. Seems odd that you've been the target of so much of it." His gaze was shrewd, his expression both curious and intense.

"I was thinking the same thing."

"Doesn't seem likely it's a coincidence, does it?"

"Not likely, but there's no proof it isn't. It's possible I've just had a round of bad luck."

"I'm not much for believing in luck, good or bad. You be careful. We don't want another Lakeview lady disappearing."

A shiver went up Raven's spine at his words. "What do you mean?"

"Just what I said. Be careful. Lakeview may be a quiet, country town, but bad things happen here, just like anywhere else. It's best to keep that in mind."

The choir began the opening hymn, interrupting the conversation before Raven could ask the questions that clamored in her mind. Sam's words had echoed Jake's, the warning to be careful chafing her already raw nerves. Did he think the things that were happening to Raven were somehow connected to the missing woman? Or were his words nothing more than a friendly reminder to be careful?

Whatever the case, the warning stayed with Raven as the service continued, and despite her best efforts to concentrate, her thoughts wandered again and again. When the sermon ended, she stood, relieved rather than renewed as she stepped out of the church with Sam.

"Deacon Parsley did a fair job preaching this week, but you'll be pleased when your brother returns. He's a man with a true calling to the pulpit."

"I'm looking forward to hearing him."

"Guess you were disappointed that he left so soon after your arrival."

"Not really—it's good that I had a chance to settle in and form my own impressions of Lakeview."

"What do you think of our town?"

"Lakeview is beautiful."

"You planning on staying a while?"

"How long I'll be here depends on how my job works out." And how her relationship with Ben progressed, but she wasn't going to share that with Sam.

"Makes sense. People often leave here to find work that pays more. Lots of them end up coming back."

"Like Thea?"

"Thea didn't leave to find work. She left because she hated this town and the people in it, and because she couldn't bear to see Daniel married to someone else. If it hadn't been for her mother's illness I don't think she would have set foot in Lakeview again."

Raven stopped walking and turned to face Sam. "She hated it that much? Why?"

"She didn't have an easy life here. Her mother never married, never told who Thea's father was. 'Course it was obvious from the looks of Thea that the man was white. That made things uncomfortable. Kind of blurred the line between one race and another. People didn't like it, and Thea got the brunt of their unhappiness."

"But she had *some* friends. You and Abby and Abby's brother."

"Now, that's true. Came from livin' on the same road, a bit away from town. We grew up together. Never saw Thea as any different than us. My parents and Abby's mother were open-minded for the times. They never tried to put a stop to the friendship, so it blossomed and thrived."

"But Abby's father felt different."

"Nathaniel Meade was a hard man. Set in his ways and not willing to bend. Too bad—things might have been different if he had. Daniel might still be around, married to Thea with a bunch of grandchildren to brag on and love."

"I'm sorry." Raven put a hand on his arm. "I shouldn't have brought it up."

"Can't blame you for being curious. Now, I've got to get home. Tori's babysitting a sick calf and I'm gonna lend a hand."

"Goodbye, Sam."

"Bye."

The story Sam had told was a sad one. Perhaps that was why Thea and Daniel lingered in Abby's mind even as everything else faded away. They lingered in Raven's mind, as well, as she drove home and as she busied herself mowing the lawn and trimming back an overgrown rosebush.

She was sure she'd dream about them and was prepared for another restless night. Instead she fell into bed, her body tired from a busy day, and slid into a deep, dreamless sleep.

The phone rang hours later, the sound shattering Raven's slumber. She sat up, her heart racing, her gaze flying to the glowing numbers on the alarm clock. Two in the morning.

Her first thought was Ben. Had he been hurt? Injured in some camping accident? He'd been fine when she spoke to him earlier in the day, but things could change so quickly. Joy could so easily be turned to anguish.

"Hello?"

"Raven? It's Shane. I'm sorry to wake you, but we've got a problem over here."

"Is Abby missing?"

"Sick. The doctor's here, trying to figure out what's wrong, but she's refusing to speak to him."

"Do you want me to come over?"

"I know it's a lot to ask, but you have a rapport with her…."

"I'll be there in a few minutes."

"I'll come pick you up."

"That would be a waste of time."

"It would also be the safe thing to do. Sit tight. I'll be there in five minutes." He hung up before she could argue.

Raven rushed to pull on jeans and a T-shirt, put on clogs, and was ready when Shane drove up. She stepped out onto the porch, snagged Merry's collar and was tugging her back toward the door when Shane walked up the steps.

"One minute. I just need to put Merry back inside."

"She can come. Abby would probably like to see her."

"You sure?"

"Yeah. Here, I'll get her." He reached down and scooped the puppy up, his arm brushing against Raven's.

The contact was brief and too welcome for her peace of mind. She hurried down the porch steps, away from Shane and all the things she longed for but knew she'd never have.

They rode to the house in silence, the absence of Shane's usual cheerful banter worrisome.

"Is Abby doing really poorly?" she finally asked.

"I'm not sure. Like I said, she's not talking," Shane said as he parked the car and pushed open the door.

Raven opened her own door and slid out. "What's the doctor saying?

"About as much as Abby. They're at a standoff." He lifted Merry from her arms and led the way into the house. "They're upstairs. In Abby's room."

Raven walked in the room behind Shane and was struck by the tension in the air. A blond man leaned against the wall, a stethoscope around his neck and a scowl on his face. Abby was in a chair, face pale, mouth set in a mutinous line. Beside her stood a short, big-boned woman who hurried forward as Shane entered the room.

"Mr. Montgomery, I'm glad you're back. I thought I'd make some tea. That might help Abby's stomach."

"Good idea, Renee, thanks."

Raven moved forward as the caregiver left. "I hear you're not feeling well, Abby. Is there anything I can do to help?"

"Thea? Is that you?"

"No. I'm Raven. We met a few days ago."

"I'm afraid I don't remember."

"That's okay. Want to tell me what's bothering you?"

Abby's dark gaze darted from Raven to the man standing against the wall. "Dr. Killjoy. He's trying to murder me."

"No, Abby, you know that isn't true. I'm your doctor. I'm here to help. Be a good girl and open your mouth so I can do the culture."

Good girl? No wonder Abby was keeping her mouth shut. Raven straightened and faced the doctor. "Why don't I do the culture? I'm sure Abby wouldn't mind."

"You're a nurse?"

"Yes. Raven Stevenson."

"Brian McMath. I'd heard Ben's sister was in town. It's nice to finally meet you."

"Thanks. You're culturing for strep?"

McMath nodded. "It's going around. She's got fever, abdominal pain, headache. And one of her caregivers had strep."

Raven remembered the feverish young woman. "I'll be happy to take care of it, Doctor."

"I doubt you'll get her to cooperate. She's being very naughty today."

"I find that patients are more willing to cooperate when they're treated with the respect and honor their age and experience deserves."

The doctor stiffened and Shane coughed. Raven glanced in his direction, saw the gleam in his eyes and the curve of his lips, and couldn't contain her own smile.

He winked, stepped forward. "Why don't you let her give it a try, Dr. McMath?"

"I doubt Abby will cooperate." He thrust out the swab, annoyance evident in the tightness of his mouth and the harsh lines of his face.

"Abby, we need to get a throat culture to check for strep. Do you mind if I do it now?"

Abby blinked but didn't respond.

"This'll only take a second. Then we'll have some tea." She opened her mouth, let Raven swab her throat.

"Thank you." Raven smiled and handed the swab to the doctor, who nodded stiffly and left the room with Shane.

"I don't like that man." Abby sounded weak, her parchment skin bleached of color.

Raven placed a hand against her brow, checking for fever as she spoke. "He *is* a little condescending."

"Who is he?"

"Dr. McMath."

"I prefer Dr. Raymond."

"I'm sorry he couldn't be here tonight."

"I haven't seen him in ages. Maybe he's gone. Maybe he's dead. So many people are. I'm the only one left." Tears streamed down her face, and Raven reached for a tissue and handed it to her.

Abby didn't use it—just sat silently, while Raven grabbed another tissue and blotted moisture from her cheeks.

"Sam's still here," said Raven. "Maybe we could invite him over for a visit one day." She hoped to draw Abby away from the past and its sorrow, but Abby was lost in her own thoughts, and seemed to hear nothing but the memories that lived in her mind. "Come on, Abby. Let's get you back in bed."

Renee appeared, a tray balanced in her hands. "How's Ms. Montgomery doing? Is she up to some tea?"

"I'm just helping her back into bed." Raven urged Abby up and over to the bed. "Would you like some tea?"

Abby turned on her side and closed her eyes.

"Has she eaten this evening?" Raven asked.

"Not that I've seen. Maybe a nibble of the chocolates her nephew brought."

"I doubt she'll touch the tea, either. I think she's sleeping." Raven pulled the comforter over Abby's thin frame.

"Don't go, Thea. It's been so long since I've seen you." Abby's eyes were open again, her voice trembling. "Daniel killed himself, you know. He was so sorry."

"I'll stay for a while." Raven pulled a chair over and held Abby's frail hand, wondering how long it would be before Abby no longer remembered her brother.

* * *

Shane rubbed his hand across his eyes as he walked up the stairs. He'd been awake since before dawn the previous day, Abby's cantankerous attitude toward her caregivers making it impossible for anyone but him to care for her properly. She'd be appalled if she realized how she was acting. He could only hope she didn't.

He passed Renee as he moved into the room and she nodded to him as she carried the tea tray out the door. Obviously Abby hadn't had any of it. Yet another worry. Still he tried to smile as he walked into the room, then he caught sight of Abby.

She'd faded even more in the past few weeks, her beautiful hair dulling, her skin drawing tight against her cheekbones. The strength that had always made her seem larger than life was gone, and only a shell of the woman remained. It hurt to see, hurt to know things would only get worse.

"Are you all right?" Raven stood, bridging the space between them and placing a hand on Shane's brow. "You feel a little warm."

"I'm fine. Just tired. It's been a long day."

"I can see that. Come and sit down." She tugged him toward the chair, waited for him to sit and then leaned forward to press her cheek against his forehead. "Definitely warm."

She smelled like flowers and spring, her skin cool and dry against his temple. What would it be like to kiss her again? This time to taste the sweetness of her lips? Shane grimaced and reined in his errant thoughts.

"Let me go get you some aspirin. Do you have a

thermometer?" She seemed oblivious to his wayward thoughts.

"In the medicine cabinet in the bathroom—but like I said, I'm fine."

Raven ignored him and hurried into the adjoining bathroom, returning moments later with a bottle of apirin and a thermometer. "Open up."

When Shane opened his mouth to protest, she thrust the thermometer under his tongue. "I—"

"No talking. Do you have a sore throat? Just nod or shake your head."

He shook his head, both amused and impressed by Raven's ability to get her patients to cooperate.

She stared at him with an I-don't-believe-you expression, and Shane could feel his throat start to ache in response.

"All right. That should be good. Let's take a look." She read the thermometer, one dark brow rising in reaction to what she saw.

"That bad, huh?"

"One hundred and two. Time for you to get in bed."

"Not possible. I've got to take care of Abby."

"Abby's asleep." She reached for his hand and tried to tug him to his feet. She was as effective as an ant trying to move an elephant.

"She won't be for long and she's not fond of poor Renee. She thinks she's in league with the doctor."

"Then I don't blame her for not liking the woman. Though I'm sure Renee is very sweet." Raven pulled harder. "You're making this more difficult than it needs to be. I'm here. I'll watch Abby while you rest."

"I can't ask you to do that."

"Why not?"

"Because you're tired and still recuperating. Because I have already asked enough of you by dragging you here to help get the throat swab done."

"I owe you, remember? I cried all over your shirt a few days ago. It's this, or I'll have to wash the shirt for you, and you know I don't have a clothes dryer."

"No. Just give me a couple of minutes and I'll drive you home."

"Don't you remember what you said to me the other day? About not being able to care for Abby if I didn't take care of myself? Isn't the same true of you? You're burning the candle at both ends. Eventually you'll run out of fuel. And then what will happen to your aunt?"

She was right. Shane knew it, but it wasn't her words that finally got him moving. It was her dark hair, lying in soft ringlets against her shoulders. Her blue eyes, so striking in her pale face. The scent of flowers that hung in the air around her. Her strength. Her determination. And the longer he stayed near her, the more tempted he was to kiss her.

He stood abruptly. "And what about you, Raven? When will you rest?"

"When you feel better. I'm used to this. Remember? Besides, Abby asked me to stay. She's thinking about the past, and I think having me here is a comfort."

"Because you remind her of Thea?"

"Maybe. I'm not sure what it is. I only know that if I can give her a measure of peace, then that's what I'm going to do. Come on, let's get some aspirin in you. Then you can sleep for a while. We'll have the doctor come back tomorrow and swab your throat."

"If I protest, will you do it instead?"

A hint of blush stained Raven's cheeks, and Shane

wondered if she were more aware of the chemistry between them than she let on.

"Take your medicine and go to bed," she ordered.

"My room's down the hall. If anything happens, come get me."

"All right."

She smiled, the gesture warm and sweet.

"You're beautiful when you smile like that." He leaned down and let his lips slide along the cool skin of her cheek. Then he turned and left.

Chapter Fifteen

For a moment Raven stood frozen in place, her hand against her cheek. She was letting Shane get too close, letting him break down the defenses she'd worked hard to erect. If she wasn't careful she'd be hurt again.

Or maybe not. Maybe Shane would prove to be all the things he seemed—kind, sweet, just a little impatient, too determined for his own good, able to love and be loved, and knowing the value of both. She shook her head against the thought, unwilling to dwell on something she didn't dare believe.

Merry padded across the threshold and Raven scratched the puppy behind her ears, forcing herself to focus on other things. She glanced around the room. The furniture was light oak, the colors bright and bold. She could imagine Abby picking the color scheme, the style, even the braided throw rug that partially hid the gleaming wood floor. Now those same things, chosen with such love and eye for detail, had become unfamiliar to her. What must it be like to slowly lose yourself? To look in the mirror and not know the face staring back at you?

Merry whined as if sensing the sadness in the air. Then she settled by Raven's feet, letting out a grunt of protest and shooting Raven a look filled with reproach.

"Sorry. These things happen. I know it's not your comfy little puppy bed, but the floor'll have to do for tonight."

And the chair would have to do for Raven. She grimaced and shifted in her seat, her eyelids heavy. She'd been wide-awake a few minutes ago, but now, with Abby's even breath whispering through the room, she felt tired.

"Can I get you anything, Ms. Stevenson?" Renee spoke from the door, her voice breaking the silence and sending Raven's heart into overdrive.

She spun to face the woman, surprised that she hadn't heard her approach. "I'm fine. Thanks."

"Is Mr. Montgomery trying to rest?"

"Yes."

"He seemed tired earlier. I offered to sit with Abby while he slept, but he didn't want her with someone she didn't know."

"It's better for patients like Abby to have familiar people around them."

Renee shrugged, all the compassion and concern she'd shown earlier gone. "I doubt it really matters to Mrs. Montgomery. You look tired. Go on home. Things are under control now."

Raven didn't like the tone of the other woman's voice. Nor did she like being ordered to leave. "Mr. Montgomery wants me to stay. I agreed."

"Suit yourself. I brought Abby some pudding. If she wakes, you should try to feed her. It won't do for her to get any thinner." She placed the bowl on the bedside table and left the room.

"Odd woman."

"Mean." Abby's eyes were open and she stared hard at Raven. "Don't eat the cake. It's poison."

"Actually, it's pudding. Would you like some?"

"Where's the book?"

"Which book?" Raven glanced at the table, saw nothing but the pudding, pitcher and empty plastic cups.

"I had to do it, you know. It's in the book." She pushed up from the bed, her frail body swaying as she stood.

"Whoa. Slow down, Abby. You can't afford to fall and break something." She put a hand on the older woman's arm and steadied her.

"We have to go find it before it's gone."

"Where are we going?"

"To the boat."

"I don't think you have a boat."

But Abby wasn't listening. Instead she moved across the room, white hair flying around her pale face, her eyes focused on some point beyond the door.

Raven hurried after her, not knowing where Abby was heading, not sure she should be allowed to go—even less sure that she should be stopped. "Where is the boat?"

"Outside."

Raven put a hand on Abby's arm, pulling her to a stop at the top of the stairs. "Let's wait until the sun comes up."

"I can't wait. Don't you see?" Her eyes beseeched Raven, begging for understanding, for help in the task she'd set for herself.

And Raven didn't have the heart to deny her. "All right. Let's go."

There was no sign of Renee downstairs, which was probably a good thing as Raven wasn't sure she had answers to any questions that might be asked. Like why she was bringing a sick patient outside at three in the morning. Raven grimaced. The fact was, she wanted Abby back in bed, tucked under the blankets and sleeping. If going outside for a few minutes would ease whatever drove the woman from slumber, then it would be well worth the trouble. But more than that, it would give Abby the right to choose, to think through what she wanted and go after it, without someone telling her no. By allowing her choices, Raven could give Abby back a small portion of the dignity her disease had stolen.

Abby didn't speak as they walked out into the night. She just moved like a wraith around the side of the house and across the few yards of grass that separated the house and the garage. She pushed open the side door and stepped through into darkness.

Raven followed, reaching for Abby's hand, wanting to keep close. "Be careful."

Inky blackness surrounded them and seemed to steal the oxygen from her lungs. She ran her hand along the wall, searching for a light switch, finding nothing. A hanging cord? Raven had never been in this part of the garage and wasn't sure if it was empty or filled. She tugged at Abby's arm, urging her to stop.

"Is there a light in here?"

Abby didn't respond, and in the silence a soft sound slid through the night. A shuffle of feet against pavement, a soft *click*, the rustle of fabric. Raven turned toward the sound, expecting to see Shane or Renee silhouetted in the doorway. Instead the door slammed shut, the sound echoing through the garage.

"Was that thunder?" Abby's arm trembled beneath her hand, and Raven tugged her closer as she turned toward the door.

"No. The door closed. It's okay. Probably just the wind." Except there wasn't any wind tonight. Not even a soft breeze had broken the stillness as they'd walked to the garage.

Raven turned the door handle and shoved at the door, but it held tight. "It's stuck. Let's find a light and see if we can figure out the problem." The words were calm, but Raven felt the hard edge of fear.

"A light? Here."

Raven let Abby lead the way through the darkness, then sighed with relief as a light burst to life.

"The boat." Abby rushed toward a covered vehicle.

"Abby, we need to go back to the house. Let's get the door open."

"Look." She pulled off the cover, revealing the long, black car beneath.

And that's when Raven smelled the smoke. It hung on the air, the acrid scent filling the room. "Abby, come on!"

She tugged Abby toward the double-wide garage door at the front of the room, placed her hand on the metal lock mechanism, and jerked back, but the heat of it was so intense she knew her fingers would blister.

"We can't get out this way. We'll have to get the other door open. Stay beside me. Don't move."

Panic made her voice sharp and her hands shake as she fumbled with the door, struggling to turn the handle. It didn't budge. She shoved her shoulder against it, slamming her weight into it, praying the old wood would give.

"Fire!"

Abby screamed the word and Raven saw flames licking at the front walls, scorching a path along dry wood.

She rammed harder against the door, felt Abby's frail

weight move with her. Thick smoke swirled around them, making every breath a burning torture.

"The stairs." Abby again, screaming instructions as her hands clawed at Raven's shirt, pulling her away from the door. Away from escape.

Some instinct urged her to go, to follow Abby through the garage to a dark corner that led nowhere. "The stairs are outside."

"And inside."

"Where, Abby? Where?"

But Abby was spinning away, coughing, running across the room back toward the car. "The book. We have to have the book."

"No. We have to get the door open. Abby…"

But she'd dived into the car, was fumbling with the backseat as Raven grabbed her around the waist and struggled to pull her from the car. Flames snaked along the walls.

"We have to get out. Are there stairs, Abby? Abby!"

And Abby spun, no longer fighting, something clutched in her hand, her eyes wild. "Somewhere. A door."

Where?

Please, God, please let me get her out of here. The prayer shouted through Raven's mind as she tugged Abby back through thick smoke, toward the side door. There were no windows on the lower level of the garage. No escape. *Was* there another door? One that led to stairs and the upper level? She felt along the wall, struggling to find her way through the gathering darkness, her feet leaden, despite the panic that surged through her.

There, in the corner, opposite the spot Abby had brought her a few moments ago—something smooth and round. A doorknob. Raven turned it, prayed the door would open, prayed they'd make it up the stairs and outside before the entire garage was engulfed in flames.

She coughed, choked on hot air as the door gave, and she and Abby stumbled into the narrow stairwell. "Come on, Abby. We have to hurry."

But there was no hurrying, only plodding steps. Up. Up through more smoke, out another door, into the kitchen. Half dragging, half carrying Abby through Shane's office. The door locked, blocked as she pushed against it. Then the window. Shoving it open, glancing down at the cool night, the grass, the flames shooting up through burning wood, lapping at her feet. Knowing it was jump or die. She took Abby's hand, pulled her close and looked into her eyes.

"We have to go out the window. It's our only chance."

Abby nodded, and a glimmer of the strong, intelligent woman she'd been sparked through the haze of uncertainty and terror.

Shane raced out the back door of the house, shouting into his cell phone, calling for help. Merry yipped and barked at his feet. Her cries had woken him from a sound sleep, woken him to the smell of smoke and the harsh crack of burning wood.

Where were Abby and Raven? Where was Renee?

He rounded the corner of the house, hoping to see them, and instead saw flames shooting up from the roof of the garage. The grass felt cool under his bare feet as he raced across the yard and into heat so intense he fell back. He righted himself, tried to see through the smoke. Something white fluttered in the garage window. Abby, white faced, leaning out. Raven behind her.

"Abby! Raven!"

Raven heard. Turned. Shouted something.

And Shane ran, ignoring the heat and the flames licking at the grass near his feet. "Jump. The whole place is collapsing." He could hear it, the creak and groan of wood warning of what would come.

"Catch her and run." Raven shouted as she lifted Abby, her movements strong, fluid, calm as she held Abby's hands, let her feet drop over the edge so Shane could grab her legs. He caught her, slid her to the ground.

"Run! Run!" Raven was scrambling out the window, yelling, her voice hoarse from smoke, terror loosening her grip.

Shane caught her as she fell, stumbled, managed to ease her down. "Was Renee with you?" He shouted over the sound of the fire.

"No."

"Let's go!" He lifted Abby and ran. The air crackled and fire roared behind them. A deafening *crash* split the air. A blast of heat. Shane was flying, falling, tumbling with Abby in his arms. Then he was up again, running, sirens screaming through the darkness, cool air replacing heat. He turned, expecting to see Raven. She was gone.

"She all right?" The words were a panicked shout.

Shane turned, saw Sam Riley racing across the grass, his granddaughter beside him. He eased Abby onto the ground, saw her eyes flutter open, then shouted to Sam and Tori, "Stay with Abby."

Then he ran back toward the flames, praying he could find Raven amidst the wreckage.

"Raven!"

* * *

"Here. I'm here." She tried to shout, but only a whisper escaped. Her throat, raw and hot, would release no more than that. Flames ate at the debris that lay around her, and she pushed aside smoldering wood, barely feeling the pain of seared skin as she freed herself and stood.

A dark figure lunged through flame and smoke, and she lurched back, afraid, disorientated.

"No. This way."

She knew the voice, reached for Shane's hand, following him through the rubble, past the blasting heat of the fire, and out into cool, clean air. She shivered, swayed, felt Shane's arms wrap around her.

"Thank God." He whispered the words against her hair, and she closed her eyes, letting him support her weight. "You okay?"

Raven tried to say yes, but her teeth were chattering too hard and she could only nod against his chest.

"Someone bring me a blanket."

Shane pulled a blanket around her arms. "You sure you're okay?"

"Yes." She managed to rasp out the words and forced herself to take a step back. It would be so easy to let him take care of her. Too easy.

Soft wails filled the silence and drew Raven's attention to Abby. The woman sat on the ground, Sam and Tori Riley on either side of her, the small book she'd taken from the car clutched to her chest, her face pale and streaked with soot.

"Abby, are you all right?"

Raven knelt beside her, ran hands along her frail arms, turned her hands up to check for burns.

Tori grabbed Raven's hands, stilling their frantic

movement. "She's okay. Sit for a minute, take a breath. Let's see how you are."

"I'm okay." But she sat back anyway, coughing, shaking, willing her heart to slow its frenzied rhythm.

People milled around her. Men, women, paramedics, firefighters, police—all shouting, running, moving, their motions dizzying. Raven closed her eyes against the onslaught of images, felt someone kneel beside her, slide a hand into hers and squeeze gently. She opened her eyes, saw Shane, and tried to smile.

"I guess there really are gallant knights."

"And beautiful damsels in distress." He ran a hand along her cheek. "Soot-covered beauties, but beauties nonetheless."

"Shane—"

"You doing okay, Raven?" Jake appeared and crouched in front of Raven, his eyes blazing in a face as hard as stone.

"Yes."

"Can you tell me what happened?"

"Abby woke, said she needed to get a book. I asked where it was and she said the boat. She seemed agitated. I thought if we found it she'd be able to sleep. I should never have let her come outside."

"This isn't your fault." Shane's voice was sharp, and Raven saw the look Jake shot in his direction.

"What happened after you went in the garage?"

Raven hurried through her account, trying to calm the tremors that ran through her body, wishing she'd never stepped outside with Abby. Jake listened, nodded a few times, but didn't interrupt. Nor did Shane, though he did drape an arm around his aunt's shoulders, drawing her close. Raven couldn't stop the longing that stabbed through her, the desire to be held, to be comforted, to have someone's arm around her.

She forced her gaze away from Shane and Abby, and focused on telling Jake the rest of what he was waiting to hear. "That's it. I opened the window and was trying to figure out how to lower Abby to the ground, when Shane saw us."

A man stepped forward as Raven finished speaking. "Sheriff?"

"Yeah."

"Looks like you were right."

"Arson?"

"Evidence is all there. Wasn't even an attempt to hide it."

The sheriff nodded. "Guess we'll know more when the fire is out. Thanks, Bill."

"Arson? That's impossible. Who'd want to burn down an old garage?" Raven could hear the weariness in Shane's voice. She felt weary, too, and wished for nothing more than a shower and her bed.

"Good question. Though a better one might be, 'Who'd want to kill one of the women inside it?'"

"What do you mean?" The question escaped, but Raven didn't need to hear the answer. It made sense. The slammed door, the fire, all three exits blocked.

But who was the target, and why?

Raven glanced at Shane and saw anger in the hardness of his face and the brightness of his eyes. Despite the emotion, his skin seemed pale, and she placed a hand against his cheek, checking for signs of fever. Then realized what she was doing and dropped her hand away.

He caught it, held on as he moved to his feet, pulling her up with him. "Looks like the fire's out. Let's check with the fire marshal, see if we can go in the house."

"Good idea. Stay here. I'll talk to him." Jake moved away, his stride long and purposeful.

As soon as he was out of earshot, Shane turned to Raven and leaned in close. "Is someone after you?"

"What?"

"Could someone be trying to get even with you? An old boyfriend? A patient? Anyone?"

Something hot and bitter stabbed at Raven's heart. She stiffened, tugged away from Shane's hand. "Do you think I'd put Abby in danger if there was?"

Shane knew he'd made a mistake. An unintentional one, but a mistake nonetheless. He hadn't meant to sound accusatory. Judging by the expression on Raven's face, he had. "That isn't why I'm asking."

But he didn't get a chance to explain further. Jake was coming toward them again, his scowl obvious even in the shadowy darkness. And flanking him on either side were Adam and Mark.

Chapter Sixteen

Raven stepped back as the three men approached, but Shane twined his fingers with hers, not willing to let her go before he explained. Unfortunately, the time for that explanation was not there.

"I told you hiring her was a mistake." Adam glared at Raven, his eyes hot with anger.

"This doesn't have anything to do with Raven."

"That's not what the sheriff said."

"What I said, Mr. Meade, is that someone is trying to hurt either Raven *or* your aunt."

"Obviously Aunt Abby isn't the target. She doesn't have any enemies. The community loves her. So does her family."

"I don't have enemies, either, Mr. Meade." Her hand trembled in Shane's, but Raven's voice was strong.

"Why don't we go inside to discuss this?" Mark suggested as he helped Abby to her feet. "You okay, Mom?"

"There was a flood. But we're fine now."

Shane almost smiled at her mistake. Water was still spewing onto the charred remains of the garage—a mini-flood of water streaming over the earth. Then he remembered the missing caregiver.

"Renee's still missing. Her car's gone, too."

"She came in after you went to bed. Then seemed to disappear. She must have left then." Raven tugged her hand away as she spoke.

"Who's Renee?" Jake's voice cut into the conversation.

"Abby's caregiver. Renee Winslow. She's supposed to be on duty from twelve to eight. Seems she decided to leave early." Shane glanced around.

"She a short, big-boned lady? Think I saw her as I was running over here." Sam gestured to the driveway. "Got in a car as I was cresting the hill. Then took off. Right, Tori?"

"Yes. We both saw her. It could be she was shirking her duty when things went bad. Maybe she got scared and ran."

Or maybe she'd had something to do with the fire. The knowledge hung in the air as they made their way to the house, Jake speaking into his radio, issuing orders, asking Shane a few questions as he began the process of tracking down the missing caregiver. By the time they settled into the living room the commotion outside had died down.

Unfortunately, the commotion inside had just begun. Shane rubbed at the ache behind his eyes as he listened to Mark and Adam argue over who would take Abby up to her room. Each insisted the job should be his. Neither had shown any desire to help in the past. If he had more energy, Shane would have gotten up and taken care of the problem. As it was, his head ached, his throat hurt and his body felt like it had been run over by a truck.

This was *not* a good time to be sick.

"Thea will help me." Abby's tone was one she'd used often when Shane was younger. It was just as effective now. Both men fell silent, glaring at one another over Abby's head.

"Mom—"

"I'm tired. You stay here and have a nice chat." She grabbed Raven's hand. "You don't mind, do you, Thea?"

"Not at all."

Raven glanced around, and Shane could see wariness in her eyes. But no one argued with Abby's preference, and the two women walked out of the room together.

Adam didn't wait long to make his unhappiness known. "I don't think that's a good idea."

"What?" Shane tried to sound like he cared.

"Letting that woman take Aunt Abby upstairs. She got her into that mess out in the garage. Abby might have been killed."

"And she wasn't because Raven used her head and got her out safely."

"She shouldn't have been out there at all."

"Aunt Abby insisted. We should be thankful Raven went with her instead of abandoning her like her care-giver did."

"I still think—"

"What you think is irrelevant." Mark's voice was weary, his eyes rimmed with fatigue. "Mom has bonded with Raven. Let her have what comfort she can. Life is hard enough for her lately. Any idea what's going on, Jake?"

"Wish I could say yes. But I've got more questions than answers. Three incidents in the past few days. The runaway car, the break-in at the cottage and the fire. They're connected. I'm just not sure how."

"But you're sure the fire is arson?"

"There's no doubt. We'll know how the doors were blocked sometime tomorrow."

"The doors won't lock or unlock without a key. They're the old-fashioned skeleton ones. Like the one in that door—" Shane gestured to the door that opened into the hall. "Usually the keys are in the keyholes."

"But not tonight."

"Doesn't seem like it."

Jake nodded, paced the room. "Someone has a bone to pick, either with Abby or with Raven. Eventually we'll find out who and why. For now, keep close tabs on Abby and call if you think of someone who might be holding a grudge against the family."

"Maybe it would be best to get Mom out of here for a while."

"You don't really think someone is after your mother, do you?" Adam barked out the question, and Shane wanted to tell him to go home. To take his frustration somewhere else.

"I don't know what to think. I only know that I don't want Mom hurt. She's not healthy and can't defend herself against this kind of threat. What do you think, Shane? You've been caring for her for a few months. Should we move her?"

"I wish I knew. She's been safe here. We've got an alarm system. As long as she's with someone trustworthy, I don't see how here is any different from anywhere else."

"I'd agree with that." Jake glanced around, and Shane knew he was looking at the windows, trying to calculate how good a defense they'd be.

"Do what you think is best, then. I'm going to head home. I've got an early meeting." Adam stalked away, his footsteps echoing in the hall as he left.

"He always this difficult?"

Shane shrugged at Jake's question. "More so than usual lately. Campaigning must be getting to him."

"I'm going up to check on Mom again. Then I'm heading out. Call me if anything comes up."

"I will."

Shane turned to Jake. "What do you think?"

"Wish I knew. Raven isn't admitting any problems. Abby doesn't seem the kind to have enemies. But there might be other motivations."

"Like money? You've been talking to Marshal."

"Wouldn't be doing my job if I didn't check out every angle. For what it's worth, I don't find much merit in the murder-for-inheritance theory. Abby'd be dead already."

"That makes me feel better."

Jake shrugged. "Take it however you want."

"Can I come in?" Raven stood in the threshold. She'd washed her face and hands, but soot still streaked her skin. "Mark's with Abby. I wanted to give them some time alone."

"Come on in. I've got a few more questions for you, then I'll give you a ride home." Jake ushered Raven to the couch, motioned for her to sit and took the chair opposite her.

Shane leaned against the fireplace mantel, not wanting to interrupt but not willing to leave. The smell of smoke hung on the air, probably from Raven's hair and clothes. A few seconds, that's all that had separated her from death. He forced his mind away from the thought. No sense dwelling on what might have happened. She was fine and so was Abby.

Jake's questions rumbled across the room. Questions about Raven's life before she moved to Lakeview. Questions about her job, the people she'd worked for, enemies she might have made. Questions about her husband. She glanced in Shane's direction as Jake mentioned Jonas, her hesitation obvious.

"I'm going to brew some coffee. Anyone want a cup?"

Both declined and Shane stepped out into the hall, knowing he was doing the right thing, but wishing he could stay and hear about her husband. He didn't bother brewing coffee, just drank a glass of water, put the cup in the dishwasher and walked back to the living room.

"You filed charges against him?"

Shane heard the question as he entered and his gaze flew to Raven. She looked tense and unhappy, her hands clenched into fists in her lap.

"Yes. A police officer encouraged me to because Jonas had been threatening me before I fell. I dropped the charges because what happened wasn't his fault. My husband had a mean streak but he wasn't physically violent. If I'd been more careful—"

"Stop blaming yourself." They both turned to Shane, but he didn't back down from the truth as he saw it. Though he did force some of the sharpness from his voice. "What happened to Micah was no more your fault than what happened to Abby."

"I don't want to have this conversation now."

"Too bad. Things happen sometimes. Things we can't control."

"If I hadn't—"

"Guilt is the easy road. Take it and you get to punish yourself by keeping distant from everyone who cares."

"That's a ridiculous thing to say." She surged up from the couch, her eyes blazing.

Shane knew he should keep his mouth shut, but something spurred him on. "Not from where I'm standing. Everytime something goes wrong you blame yourself and back away. You say you don't want to hurt people, but the truth is, you're afraid to be hurt."

Raven didn't speak, but her expression conveyed everything she was feeling—anger, hurt, fear. She stared at Shane for a moment, then turned and left the room.

"Nice going."

Shane whirled, ready to let off some of his frustration, but there was something in Jake's eyes that said he understood. The anger seeped out of Shane as quickly as it had entered.

"I'm an idiot."

Jake shrugged. "We're all idiots sometimes. Especially around women we care about."

"I—"

"Don't bother. I won't buy it."

"She needs someone to care, she just won't admit it."

"She's got Ben. I've already called him. He's taking the first flight home."

"You think she'll be happy about that?"

"I think she'll have her brother here in case something else happens."

"She's got me, too."

"So tell her." Jake stood, rolling his shoulders and neck. "It's been a long night. I'm heading home. Tiffany'll be up waiting. Wondering why I'm not there yet. Worrying that something's happened."

"Must be nice."

"Yeah. It is. But it isn't something I thought I'd ever have. Isn't something I thought I deserved. I met Tiffany and knew she was special, but it took a while longer to realize God had plans for me and her, plans that meant giving up my fears and trusting in Him. Raven's like I used to be, wanting to control life because she's afraid of hurting or being hurt."

"That sounds right."

"When she learns to trust God and herself, she'll be able to trust other people. So pray for her, be there for her. And wait. There's nothing else you can do. I'll call when we have news. Stay safe." And he was gone.

Shane walked to the window and stared out into the lightening world, wondering if Raven was okay, if he should go after her and apologize. Wondering if Jake was right, if the only thing that stood between them was her lack of trust. He didn't know. He could only hope that in His time, in His way, God would reveal His plan for their lives. With that in mind, he took Jake's advice, and began to pray.

Raven stood on the porch, tired, shivering, angry. When the door opened she didn't turn.

"You ready to go?" Jake's voice broke the silence.

"Yes."

"You sure?"

"What do you mean?"

"Shane's got a big mouth, but he means well."

"I know."

"Then why'd you walk out?"

Raven didn't answer. What could she say? That Shane had been right. That it had hurt to hear the truth? That she was a coward, too afraid of what she saw in Shane's eyes to stay?

"Might be best if you stayed. For Abby and for you."

"I'd think the opposite—that if we're apart it'll be easier to figure out who the real target is."

"That's true, but there's strength and safety in numbers."

"There wasn't earlier." She glanced at the debris that littered the yard.

"Only because you weren't on guard. Now you will be."

"What do you want me to say, Jake? We both know I'd be pretty useless at protecting Abby."

"I want you to say you'll stay here today. It would make me feel better if you didn't go back to the cottage. At least until we track down the missing caregiver."

"Do you think I'm the target?"

"I don't know. What I do know is this house has an alarm system, yours doesn't. You'll be safer here."

Raven wanted to argue, but she knew he was right. Despite her rush from Shane's presence, she had no desire to go back to the empty cottage. At least not until the sun was high and bright and the shadows gone.

"I have to find my puppy anyway, so I guess it wouldn't hurt to stay for a while."

"That's the homely little rat dog, right?"

"She's cute, kind of, but her tail is a little ratty looking."

"Saw her inside a while ago."

"I'll go see if I can find her."

Jake stepped down off the porch. "Take care."

"I will. And thanks."

He nodded and waved as he left.

Raven turned back to the house, stepped into the hallway and saw Shane. "I've lost Merry."

"Last time I saw her, she was heading upstairs."

"I'll go find her." She moved toward the steps, but

wasn't surprised when he put a hand on her arm, holding her in place.

"I'm sorry. Sometimes my mouth runs a lot faster than my brain."

"And sometimes I'm defensive, even when I shouldn't be. So I guess we're even."

"Guess so. Does that mean you forgive me?"

"There's nothing to forgive."

Shane smiled, slid his hand around Raven's. She winced as his fingers brushed against tender skin.

"You're hurt." He pulled her hand up and examined the blistered flesh on her palm. "Why didn't you say something when the ambulance was here?"

"It didn't hurt until now. Too much adrenaline pumping through me for a little pain to register." She shrugged and would have pulled away, but he didn't loosen his hold. She glanced up. There were questions in Shane's eyes. Questions he wouldn't ask. Questions about what she wanted, what she'd accept from him.

And she wanted everything. Wanted to trust him with her feelings, wanted to believe he really was the knight in shining armor rushing to the rescue. She couldn't, though. It would hurt too much if it turned out the armor was tarnished and the knight nothing more than a rogue in disguise.

He seemed to sense her reservations and released her hand. "Let's go see if we have some ointment for your hand. There are gauze pads in the medicine cabinet."

Raven followed him up the stairs. She felt weary suddenly, as if her legs would no longer hold her weight.

Shane knocked on Abby's door and stepped inside. Abby was where Raven had left her, tucked in bed, with Mark sitting vigil by her side. He looked up as they entered, smiling sheepishly as he placed the empty pudding bowl back on the bedside table.

"I ate Mom's pudding."

"I don't think she'll miss it. She hasn't eaten much at all lately." Shane stepped close to the bed and his eyes filled with sadness.

Raven wanted to put a hand on his shoulder, tell him to sit down and take a break from his worry.

She didn't. It wasn't her right to say anything and so she kept silent—just watched while he wiped a smudge from Abby's cheek.

"You sticking around for a while, Mark?"

"I need to get back home. I'll stop by tomorrow after work. If you need me, give me a call."

"All right."

Shane ran a hand over his forehead and winced. Mark didn't seem to notice, but Raven did, and as the two men said goodbye, she walked into the bathroom and grabbed the bottle of aspirin, took two out and brought them into the bedroom.

"Here, take these."

"Thanks. Now, let's find that puppy."

As if on cue, Merry peeked out from under the bed, her tongue lolling.

"There you are. I've been wondering. Too much confusion, eh?" Raven knelt down and scratched the puppy behind her ears, smiling as Merry slipped out from under the bed.

"I'd offer to give you a ride home, but I'd rather not wake Abby."

"It's okay. Jake said he wanted me stay here for a little longer. Do you mind?"

"No. I'm getting kind of used to having you around."

He smiled, his eyes filled with something Raven had to turn away from.

"What are you going to do about your writing? Everything's been destroyed."

"Changing the subject?"

She turned back, saw he'd knelt down beside her and was just inches away. "You're making this personal." She gestured toward Abby. "It isn't."

"It feels personal. Can you say any different?"

"I don't *want* anything personal. I agreed to help care for Abby because she seems comfortable with me and because it's what I've been trained to do. Anything more than that is something I won't allow."

He watched for a moment, silent, solemn. Then he nodded. "My writing isn't a problem. I send copies of my files to my home computer and to my laptop. Nothing's lost that can't be found again."

"I'm glad."

"I'm going to find the gauze and ointment for your hand. After that we both should try to get some sleep. There are two guest rooms. You're welcome to either."

"I'll use that fold-up cot. That way if Abby wakes I'll be here."

"I'll do that."

"If I'm staying I'd like to be useful. Besides, what if you have strep and Abby doesn't? It would be better to keep your distance until you know for sure."

"I'd argue, but I feel worse than I have since I had mono my senior year of high school." He stepped into the bathroom, returned a moment later, and handed Raven gauze, tape and antibiotic cream. "Let me see your hand." He bent over the blistered skin and slathered ointment across the stinging flesh.

Raven sucked in a breath.

"Sorry." Shane glanced up, and Raven caught her breath again.

He looked pale, tired, and more handsome than any man had a right to be. She wanted to brush the hair away from his brow, to let her fingers linger against his skin.

That, more than anything, made her pull her hand back. "I'll do the gauze."

For a moment she thought he'd refuse. His eyes flashed irritation and something else, something knowing. Then he handed her the gauze. "I'm going to set the alarm. Then I'm lying down."

He was gone before Raven could say anything. She finished wrapping her hand, pulled out the cot, turned off the light and lay down. Merry jumped up and curled near her knees, and Raven let her hand drift along the dog's warm fur.

"I should make you get down, you know."

But her hand throbbed, her body ached and she felt more lonely than she had in years, so she let the puppy stay as she watched sunlight slowly drift across the ceiling of the room.

Chapter Seventeen

The dream came and she was running, racing down the hall, fleeing from Jonas and his hate. Fire raced with her, eating at the walls, licking at her feet, and she realized Abby was beside her. They ran together, tumbling over the first step, falling into nothingness.

Raven jerked upright, her heart pounding, her breath ragged, her gaze flying to the other bed. Abby was still there, sleeping deeply, a flush staining her cheeks. Fever? Raven scrambled up from the cot, upending Merry who slid to the floor with a disgruntled bark.

"Sorry, mutt."

Abby's brow felt warm to the touch and Raven rooted through the medicine cabinet, searching for dissolvable tablets. She found them and hurried back into the room.

"Abby?"

The older woman moaned, opening her eyes and gazing at Raven with fever-bright eyes. "Thea? What are you doing here?"

"I've brought you something for your fever."

"You can't be here. I left you near the tree."

"I came back."

"It was the baby. Everything would have been fine otherwise."

Raven froze at her words, wondering what they meant, how they were connected to Thea's disappearance. "Thea's baby?"

"It would have been a beautiful baby."

"Is that why Thea left? So people wouldn't know?"

"There's a tree in the cemetery. I wonder if I can find it?" Abby allowed Raven to slip a tablet into her mouth, her eyes drifting closed.

"It's okay, Abby. Whatever you need to find, I'll help you."

"Will you?" Abby's eyes flew open, tears falling and washing over the heated flesh of her cheeks.

"Of course. Just tell me."

"Two crosses. Not there but close. It's been so long, I don't know if I can find it by myself. But it's time. It was time long ago, but I didn't want to hurt anyone. Didn't want people to think poorly of you. It was so important to you."

"You were a good friend, Abby. Thea knew that."

"Sin is sin." And then she slid down under the covers, closed her eyes and drifted back to sleep.

Raven let her hand rest on Abby's frail shoulder. Did Abby sense that she was drifting away? Slowly but surely heading toward eternity?

A phone rang, the sound muted but insistent, drawing Raven's thoughts away from the sadness of Abby's life. Footsteps sounded in the hall, a door snapped shut, then there was silence again. Time passed and Raven sat vigil, watching for signs that Abby's fever was worsening.

She wasn't surprised when the bedroom door swung

open. Some part of her had been expecting it. Had known that once he woke Shane would be here.

"That was Dr. McMath. Abby does have strep. He's calling in a prescription for her and one for me, as well."

"Without examining you?" She turned, met his gaze.

"Said I have classic symptoms and it's better to treat us both. I think he doesn't want to be bothered doing another culture." He ran a hand through his hair and tried to smile. His skin was pale, his cheeks flushed and a lock of dark hair fell across his brow.

"You need to rest for a while longer."

"Can't. It's almost nine. I need to call the insurance company, get someone out here to look things over. Then run to the pharmacy and pick up the prescription. We're out of chocolate ice cream and it's the only thing Abby eats. Plus I don't think we have any other food in the house. I meant to go to the store two days ago, but things didn't work out."

"I can do all those things. You have your policy number and the company phone number?"

"Got it out earlier."

"I'll make the call, then run to the store to get groceries and the medicine. By tomorrow you and Abby will be feeling better." She stood and started to move by Shane.

He put a hand on her shoulder, the heat of his skin searing through the cotton of her T-shirt. "Careful, Raven, you don't want to make yourself too useful."

"Being useful is part of the job." Raven tried to make light of the moment, but Shane didn't smile. Just stared down at her, his eyes deep green, his hand easing along her shoulder and cupping the nape of her neck.

"You're more than useful. You're compassionate,

hardworking and very lovely. I could go on, but you're blushing."

"It's warm in here."

"Is it?" He skimmed his palm up to her jaw, traced the line of her cheek with his finger.

"Shane, I—"

"Don't worry, I'm too sick to steal a kiss." He smiled, but the look in his eyes said he wasn't joking.

Before Raven could comment or pull away, Abby shifted and opened her eyes, her gaze surprisingly alert. "Well, it's about time. I didn't think you'd ever get married."

"How're you feeling, Aunt Abby?"

"Happy. I wanted to see you married before I die."

"You aren't going to die. Not yet anyway."

"Everyone dies. It's part of life."

"Yeah, but since Raven and I aren't married, you're going to have to wait to make your journey to the other side."

"Not married?"

"Nope."

"You're acting like you are."

"Since when is touching someone's cheek acting married?"

"Since I saw the look in your eyes."

Raven cut in before Shane could comment. "Shane's not feeling well. That's fever you see in his eyes."

"You're sick?" Abby shifted and sat up, reaching to feel Shane's forehead. "You'd better get in bed."

"I'm fine, Aunt Abby."

His words didn't seem to register. Abby turned to Raven. "If you marry him you'll have to keep him in line. He likes to do things." She stopped, looked confused.

"I write books. And you're jealous because I've got more talent than you. Now lie back down. You've got strep. The doctor said you need to rest."

"When are you getting married? You're not letting him stall, are you?"

Heat bathed Raven's cheeks as Abby and Shane both gave her their full attention. "I…don't know."

"Christmas Eve," said Shane. "Raven's going to wear a long, pale gown and a crown of flowers. I'll be in black tie with a ribbon from her hair tied around my arm. We'll have the ceremony at the church, then borrow that old white pony from Sam Riley and the fancy cart he has. Ride back here for a big party to celebrate."

"Oh! Lovely. We have to go shopping. I'll need a dress." She looked down at the loose flannel nightshirt she wore. "And I need to eat. I can't look like a scarebird at the wedding."

"Which is why Raven is going to the store to buy food and you're going to rest. You need to stay healthy."

"Yes." She closed her eyes, a smile curving her lips, her expression more relaxed and happy than Raven had ever seen it.

"Shane, you shouldn't have told her that," she whispered, not wanting to disturb Abby.

"Why not?"

"You lied to her. Just because she might not remember, doesn't mean she won't. And look how much it means to her. Look how happy she is."

"She probably will remember. I hope she does remember. As far as I'm concerned it isn't a lie."

"What?"

"It's what I want. Maybe not this Christmas, but one Christmas."

"That's fine. Spinning a tale about your wedding is wonderful. Just don't put me in it."

"Sorry. Without you, there is no tale." The truth of it was in his eyes—all the promises he wouldn't give, all the things he'd like to say but wouldn't because she wouldn't let him.

Raven backed toward the door. "Should I leave Merry here, or bring her back to the cottage?"

"Leave her. I'll let her out. Come on. I need to turn off the alarm before you open the door." He draped an arm around her shoulders, the gesture so easy, so right, she couldn't protest.

Still, she couldn't allow him to forget the truth of who she was and what she wanted. "I'm never getting married again. Once was enough for me."

"Okay."

"I mean it."

"I know."

"You're going to have to find some other woman for your Christmas Eve fantasy."

"Not possible. The story's already been told, can't change it now."

"Are you always this obstinate?" Raven glared at him as he punched in the code to the alarm system.

"Yes. Are you?"

She laughed and shook her head. "Only when it matters."

"Then we should make a good team. Here—" He reached into his pocket, pulled out a wallet and handed her a thick fold of cash. "Buy what you want. There's a pharmacy at the grocery store. That's where the prescription will be. And take my car. Here are the keys. I don't want you walking back to the cottage."

"What about the insurance company?"

"I'll make the call, then rest once it's taken care of."

"Anything special I should bring back?"

"Chocolate ice cream, the medicine—and you."

Raven was smiling as she walked down the porch steps and into bright morning sun.

It didn't take long to pick up the prescription and buy some groceries. She returned to the Montgomery house two hours later, and was surprised to see a beat-up pickup truck and a motorcycle parked in the driveway. Merry raced around the side of the house to greet her, and Raven let the bags tumble from her hands as another dog bounded after the puppy. Big, black and weighing a hundred pounds at least, he looked like he could eat Merry in one gulp.

"Stop!" Raven ran toward the dog, and was surprised when it skidded to a stop a few feet from her. "Good. Now go home. Merry is a dog, not Puppy Chow. You can't eat her."

"I don't think he planned to. Though I can understand why you'd worry." A tall woman with golden red hair and an open, friendly smile had come around the side of the house. "I'm Tiffany Reed. Jake's wife."

"Nice to meet you. And your dog."

"That's Bandit. I adopted him last summer. He's big, but harmless. He and Merry were playing." She held out her hand. "You must be Raven."

"That's right."

Before either could say more, Jake stepped onto the porch, nodded at Raven and smiled at his wife. The expression changed him and Raven could see how love made him softer. "All set, Tiff. Sorry to hold up the plans."

"No sweat. The fabric store will still be there."

"I know, but we've been planning this for a while and things keep coming up. I want to keep my promise to you."

"And you are." Tiffany linked hands with Jake and smiled as he bent to kiss her.

Raven felt like an interloper and turned away, uneasy in the face of their love for one another. She bent to pet Merry and Bandit, pretending she hadn't felt a twinge of envy at the affection between the couple.

"You have any problems in town?"

She turned back to face Jake. "No. Everything was fine."

"Good. Just stay alert. I don't like how things are shaping up. I've got patrols driving by, but that won't help if someone's determined to cause trouble."

"I'll be careful. Did you find Renee?"

"No. The agency she works for hasn't heard from her, either. We got her address, checked her house—looks like she packed up and left. We're trying to trace her now. Once we find her, we'll have answers. There's more. Shane will fill you in. If you have questions or concerns call the station. I'll be back on shift tomorrow. We've got to head out. Stay safe."

"Thanks. It was nice meeting you, Tiffany."

"You, too. Hopefully we'll have more time to chat next time." They got in the truck, Bandit jumped in the back and they took off.

"Come on, girl. Let's go see what news Shane has." She scooped Merry up, picked up the bags she'd dropped and walked into the house.

Voices were coming from the kitchen and she followed the sound, stepping into the scent of vanilla and sweet bread. Shane sat at the kitchen table, a pencil in one hand, the phone to his ear. He looked up as Raven entered the room, smiling in her direction, his cheeks still flushed with fever. Something warm wove its way through her heart and she turned from his gaze, finally noticing the man standing by the stove. "Ben!"

He set down the pan he was holding and moved across the room. "How're you doing?"

"I'm fine. What are you doing home? I thought you weren't getting back until Friday." She stepped into his arms, allowed herself to be hugged.

"Only two more days. I cut the trip short."

"I'm glad you're back, but you shouldn't have come on my account."

"How do you know that's why I'm back early?"

"You're Jake's friend. He probably called you this morning. You got worried, took the first plane back and came looking for me."

"Guilty. But we can talk about that after I get the cinnamon buns out of the oven."

"Homemade?" Raven reached into one of the grocery bags and pulled out the chocolate ice cream.

"Yep. Got here a few minutes after you left, so I figured I'd make myself useful. Now, no talking. I'm not a multitasker and I'd hate to mess up the glaze. It's the best part." He turned, and Raven mouthed *bossy* at his back. Then she caught Shane watching, a grin tugging the corners of his mouth.

She shoved the ice cream into the freezer and pulled from a bag the medicine bottles she'd picked up. "Time to get healthy. Abby first, then you, Shane."

"Do I get a spoonful of sugar with that?" Shane winked as Raven handed him a pill and a glass of water.

"How about a glass of juice instead?" Ben filled a

glass and set it in front of him, and Raven saw the way his gaze traveled from Shane to her.

If he noticed anything, if he could feel the connection between them, he didn't comment. Just went back to the counter and slathered white glaze on hot rolls.

"They're getting married, you know." Abby's voice drifted into the silence, and Raven's hand froze on the box of rice she was putting in the cupboard.

"Ben, you didn't tell me how your reunion was," she said quickly.

"It was great. I've got plenty of photos. Sit down and have a roll—they're best when they're fresh out of the oven." He slid a plate in front of Shane, one in front of Abby, then one at each of the two extra places.

Raven sat and fiddled with the edge of a napkin, hoping the subject of marriage would be dropped. "And were your mom and dad happy to see you?"

"Thrilled. So, who's getting married?"

Raven choked on a bite of cinnamon bun and felt the firm, smooth slap of Shane's hand against her back as he spoke.

"I'm planning a Christmas Eve wedding, but Raven's not quite ready to commit."

"At Grace Christian Church?"

"Yeah."

"Candlelight?"

"Hadn't thought about it, but it sounds good to me."

Raven finally managed to stop her coughing long enough to get a word out. "No!"

"You don't like candles anymore, Rae? You used to love them when we were kids." Ben took a bite of roll, his eyes glinting with amusement.

"It's not funny. I'm not getting married again. Not ever."

"That's a long time." This time Ben looked more serious, but seemed disinclined to continue the conversation. "Are you going to eat, Ms. Abby? Let me help you with that." He used a fork to stab a piece of sweet bread and fed Abby a bite.

"Do I know you?" Abby picked up the roll and took another bite.

"I'm Ben Avery. Pastor at the church you attend. Also Raven's brother."

"How nice. It's wonderful to have a brother. My brother's gone."

"I'm sorry. That must be painful."

Raven let the sound of their conversation drift over her, allowed herself to enjoy the warmth of the room, the comfort of knowing people who cared were nearby.

"You two are a lot alike." Shane spoke in a low tone, his voice not breaking into the quiet rhythm of Ben and Abby's conversation.

"He's much kinder than I am."

"No. I don't think so." Shane yawned, pushed his half-eaten roll away. "Sorry, that was delicious, Ben, but I'm beat. Hopefully the medicine will kick in soon. For now, though, I think I might need some more sleep. How about you, Abby—want to take a nap?"

"I *am* tired. Let's watch the thing."

"Television? You can watch while you rest."

"That would be lovely."

"Do you want me to go with her?" Raven started to stand, but Shane shook his head, his eyes warning that there was more to his fatigue than illness.

"Actually, I want to get Abby settled, then there are a few things I need to speak with you about."

"I'll wait, then."

He led his aunt out of the kitchen and Raven stood to collect the plates.

"Let me get that." Ben pulled the dishes from her hands. "Sit down. You look exhausted."

"You're being bossy again." But she sat anyway.

"It's a tough job, but someone's got to do it."

"I wish you hadn't come home. I feel terrible that you cut your reunion short because of me."

"I cut it short because I wanted to. Because you're my sister and I'm worried."

"I'm sorry."

"Why? Nothing that happened is your fault." Ben sat down next to her, his eyes so blue, so filled with understanding, it almost hurt to look in them.

"Funny, that's what Shane said last night."

"Shane was right. So tell me, what's between you two?"

"I don't know. Some fantasy he's cooked up about a knight, a damsel in distress and happily ever after." If her voice sounded wistful Raven refused to hear it.

"Sounds nice."

"*Sounds* nice. But reality is a lot different. Reality is people falling out of love. People who thought they'd have a forever having a year or two, or ten."

"You had a bad marriage. Not everyone does."

"I know, but I'm not willing to chance another mistake."

"Maybe you should be. Not everyone should spend life alone."

"You do."

"Because I'm content with my life the way it is. I have my ministry, my faith, my friends…and now you. That's enough."

"Did you love your wife?"

Ben was silent, the sadness in his eyes making Raven regret the question.

"Sorry. I'm prying. Forget I asked."

"No. It's okay. I did love my wife. Theresa and I didn't get forever, but the years we had were great."

"I'm glad. It must be wonderful to have that kind of marriage."

"It is. I wouldn't trade the time we had for anything."

"But you don't want to marry again? Have that kind of relationship again?"

He shrugged. "Like I said, my life is full."

"So is mine."

"Is it?"

The question hung between them, the answer still unspoken as Shane stepped back into the room.

Chapter Eighteen

"You guys look serious."

"Just having a family powwow, right, Rae?"

"Right."

"Sorry to break up the discussion, but Abby is quiet for a bit and I wanted to talk to you when she wasn't around. I can never tell how much she's taking in and I don't want to scare her."

"What's going on?" Raven's pulse leaped at his tone, remembered fear making her throat dry.

"I got a call from Mark's wife a few minutes after you left. She was at the emergency room with him. He fell asleep at the wheel on the way home."

"Oh, no! Is he okay?"

"Just some minor bruising. Problem is, the doctors were having trouble waking him. They did a blood test and found a sedative in his system."

"Did he take something?"

"He says no and I believe him."

"The pudding," Raven said, and Shane nodded.

"That's what I'm thinking and what Mark was thinking."

"Is there any way to be sure?"

"Jake took the dish. They'll do some tests, see what they find."

"But why sedate Abby?"

"Could be someone had a reason for making sure she was asleep. Could be that person was hoping the sedative would do *more* than just make her sleep."

"But why?"

"Good question. Wish I had an answer."

"At least we know she's the target. We can take extra precautions and make sure she's never alone."

"We will. But Jake still isn't convinced Abby is the target. He said it could just as easily be someone trying to harm you. What better way to hurt a nurse than to damage her reputation?"

"Wouldn't I know it if someone hated me enough to hurt me in that way?"

"Probably, but there's no sense taking chances. Ben and I were talking and we think it would be best if you didn't stay at the cottage alone."

"I wish you'd included me in the discussion."

"We are now."

"Then I'll give you my opinion. I'm perfectly capable of taking care of myself, and I'll be fine at the cottage by myself."

"No one said you couldn't take care of yourself. The question is, are you safe being alone?" Shane's voice and eyes were hard, frustration underlying the words.

"I'll be—"

"Shane's right," Ben cut in smoothly. "This isn't about your ability to take care of yourself. It's about safety. Until Jake can figure out what's going on and catch the person responsible, I'd like to stay at the cottage with you."

"I can't ask you to do that, Ben."

"You're not asking—I'm offering. Besides, I won't rest easy until the situation is resolved."

Raven shrugged, not sure she liked the idea, but knowing it would be best to err on the side of caution. "We can put a bed in the upstairs room."

"Good. Then I'll go now, get a few things together and meet you at the cottage later." He pressed a kiss to the top of her head and said goodbye to Shane.

Shane turned to Raven. She looked tired and scared, though he doubted she'd admit to either. "How's your hand feeling?"

"It hurts, but I've felt worse. Oh—" she dug in her pocket and pulled out some money "—your change."

"Thanks." He took the money, trying to ignore the warmth of her fingers as they brushed his.

"Are you still feverish?"

"I took some aspirin. I'll be fine." The conversation felt stilted, and everything Shane wanted to say seemed like too much, too soon. "My problem is, I'm an all-or-nothing kind of guy."

"What?" Raven's eyebrows went up, but her mouth hinted a smile.

"My father raised me to say it like it is. I try to curb that, but I'm not always successful."

"I don't mind."

"I know. That's one of the things I like about you. You aren't offended by my honesty, and you'll argue with me if you think I'm wrong."

"Some people would find that annoying."

"I'm not one of them." He reached for Raven's hand and pulled her to her feet. "Look, I don't have any better way to do this and I'm just not made to pretend. I admire you. I'm attracted to you. I think both those things are obvious."

Raven stiffened at his words but didn't pull her hand away. "Yes. They are."

"So here's the deal. I know you've been through a rough time. Your marriage was terrible. You lost a child and you blame yourself for that loss. You've come to Lakeview to get to know your brother, and I don't think you're interested in relationships beyond that."

"That's true."

"I just want you to know that I have time. Lots of it. I'm in no hurry. When you're ready to move on with your life, I'll be here. And if you're never ready, I won't push you for what you can't give."

"Shane—"

"Shh." And as he had earlier, he put his finger against her lips, felt the warmth of her breath, the smoothness of her skin. "I'm the gallant knight, remember? Being patient, understanding and heroic is what I do."

"I need to go home. I smell like smoke—" Her voice broke and she hurried from the room.

"Take my car and be careful, Raven."

"Thanks. I'll be back tomorrow. Eight a.m."

"See you then."

She stepped outside, got in the car and drove away.

As the car drove out of sight, Shane turned and went back into the house. Much as he might like to play the part of gallant and courageous knight, right now he felt tired, sick and lonely. That surprised him. He'd been content with his life until Raven showed up. Now it took everything he had to keep from calling her back and trying to convince her that love could be much sweeter than she'd found it the first time around.

Abby and her husband, Ethan, had been a good example of that kind of love. Their relationship had been constant, abiding and supportive. Shane could remember visiting them, seeing the strength of their love and wondering if he'd ever have that. Now he was beginning think he might. *If* he could get Raven to believe in him. He smiled as he remembered her face when Abby announced that they were getting married. The next few months should be interesting.

Hopefully they wouldn't prove deadly, as well.

Who was the target? Abby or Raven? It didn't seem possible that either could be. Yet it was obvious someone wanted to hurt one of them. Shane closed the door and set the alarm. He had too many questions and not enough answers. For now he needed to rest, and regain his health and strength. Then he'd find out who attacked Raven and Abby.

When he did, someone would pay.

The next few days passed uneventfully. Raven worked with Abby during the day and returned home at night, always accompanied by Ben whether she drove or walked to the Montgomery house. She'd thought it would be difficult to have him at the cottage. The opposite was true. Late at night, when she woke from nightmares with the sound of old wood creaking and groaning around her, it was nice to know she wasn't alone. Though Ben sometimes asked probing questions he didn't press for answers, and he let her have privacy and solitude.

No, Ben wasn't a problem. It was Shane who worried Raven. Shane, who seemed to take up too much of her thoughts.

And he wasn't even trying.

True to his word he hadn't pushed for more than she wanted to give. As a matter of fact, he seemed barely aware of Raven's presence, exchanging pleasantries with her when they came in contact with one another, but no more than that. It shouldn't have bothered her. It did.

"You almost ready? Won't do for the pastor to be late for church." Ben peeked into the open door of her room.

Raven dragged a brush through her hair, pulled the curls into a tight chignon and stepped from the bedroom. "Ready."

"Wow! My sister's all grown up and a knockout. I'm not sure I feel comfortable with that." Ben grinned and pushed the front door open, nudging Merry aside with his toe. "Go to bed, pup, we'll be home soon."

Merry looked crestfallen but obeyed, climbing into the doggy bed Raven had bought her.

"How'd you do that? She never listens to me unless I've got a treat."

"You're too soft and she knows it. Come on. I was going to give you a ride on the motorcycle, but I think we'll save that for a day when you're dressed more appropriately."

"Good plan. I don't want people at church to think your sister doesn't know how to make a good impression."

"The only thing that matters to me is that you're back in my life. That you've turned into a wonderful Christian woman. A woman I'll be proud of, no matter what anyone else thinks. Which reminds me, I bought you something."

He handed her a Bible, the leather cover smooth under her fingers as she took it.

"I know yours was stolen and you haven't had a chance to get a new one."

"This is wonderful, Ben. Thanks."

"No problem. Now let's get going."

Despite Ben's comment about being late, they arrived early and walked into an almost empty church. Their footsteps echoed in the hall as they moved toward the offices, and Raven wondered if her brother's house was as empty when he was there alone. He'd said he was content with his life and happy with his work and friends, but did he ever want more?

"You really don't think you'll ever remarry?"

"I doubt it. This is my life now. There isn't room for anything else."

"You could make room."

Ben stopped and turned to face her. "If God wants something else for my life He's going to have to drop it in my lap, or beat me over the head with it. Otherwise, I'm content to keep doing what I'm doing. Now, I'm going to have a few minutes of quiet time before service begins."

Raven sighed and stepped into the sanctuary. A few people had arrived before her and were scattered among the pews, heads bowed in prayer. The weight of their struggles hung in the air, the need to connect with God charging the atmosphere. Raven edged back toward the door, feeling like an intruder, a shadow hanging at the edge of things she couldn't quite understand.

She meant to leave and instead found herself moving forward, the urge to seek her own answers and her own peace pulling her toward the back pew. She took a seat and bowed her head, listening to the silence and to the sound of her own heartbeat. If there were answers she couldn't find them. If there was a way to fill the emptiness inside her, she didn't know it.

Behind her the doors to the sanctuary opened and voices drifted into the quiet. People arrived chatting, laughing, eager for fellowship. Raven didn't move, didn't look up. The guilt and anger she'd harbored for so long gnawed at her mind.

As the service began she stood, sang, prayed, listened, went through the motions of worship, but found comfort in none of it. Her hands trembled as she opened the Bible and read the passage Ben was speaking on. The love verses. She'd memorized them long ago.

"Love is patient, love is kind. It does not envy, it does not boast, it is not proud. It is not rude, it is not self-seeking, it is not easily angered, it keeps no record of wrongs. Love does not delight in evil but rejoices with the truth. It always protects, always trusts, always hopes, always perseveres. Love never fails."

But it *had* failed, hadn't it?

Wasn't Micah's death proof that God's love was as fickle as the love of the people He'd created? He could have prevented her son's death. He hadn't, though He'd known how much she longed for the child she was carrying. The anger inside her surged and receded, pushing and prodding at her tired spirit.

She looked up and saw her brother strong and confident, despite the hardships he'd endured. For a moment their eyes met, and she knew he understood, that he'd seen in her the same kind of anger that had once driven him from his faith.

Her hands shook as she closed the Bible and stood, hurrying from the sanctuary and outside into the bright, spring sun. She crossed the parking lot, moved into the trees that separated the church from Ben's house. A cool breeze rustled the leaves, reminding Raven of her first day in Lakeview, of the music of the country, the sweet fragrance of clean air that had been so new, so alive with possibilities.

"You okay?"

Raven turned toward the voice, her heart leaping as she saw Shane, his dark hair carefully combed, his eyes as green as the spring that bloomed around them.

"I needed some air."

He nodded, as if leaving church before the service ended was the most natural thing in the world.

"Is Abby here today?"

"Mark is at home with her. Her immune system is still shaky and we don't want her contracting something else."

"And you're feeling better?"

"Much. How about you?"

"I'm fine." She turned, pulling a fragrant leaf from a branch and letting it twirl and dance to the ground.

"That's not true and we both know it. But I won't push for answers. I won't ask why you walked out of church. Why you're standing here all alone."

But he wanted to and the knowledge burned between them, the boundaries Raven had erected standing firm, despite the fact she didn't know if she wanted them there any more.

"Let's go back inside together."

He held out his hand and Raven took it, enjoying his strength as he led her back through the trees and into the sunlight. Then he released his hold and stepped away.

She wanted to pull him back, wanted to tell him all the things she was thinking, all the secrets of her heart, wanted to trust him, trust herself, trust that God would take all the anger, the guilt, the fear in her and make it into something beautiful.

A tear slid down her cheek and she turned away from Shane, not wanting him to see what was in her eyes.

But he did. She felt his hands on her shoulders, urging her around. Then she was in his arms, pressed close to his heart. He loosened his hold, looked down into her face, then backed away, wiping the tear from her cheek and smiling, though there was sadness in his eyes.

"We need some time to think, Raven. Both of us. What I feel for you isn't changing, it's just becoming more. If you don't feel the same, I understand, but I can't keep seeing you day after day, pretending that there's nothing between us."

"I know." And she did.

"Take a week or two off. Give us both some distance from each other. Then we'll talk. See where we stand. Maybe I'll come to my senses and stop imagining you at that Christmas Eve wedding."

"Shane—" She wanted to tell him she didn't need time. That she saw in his eyes everything she'd longed for. Fear held back the words, the bitter knowledge that she'd believed in love once and learned a hard lesson stopping her from saying what she knew was true.

Coward. She could almost hear the word, though Shane didn't speak it. It floated through her mind, mocking her as people began to stream from the church, as Shane took a step away, and then another. Until finally she was left alone. An island of aloneness, with only herself to blame.

Chapter Nineteen

Three days later, Raven paced the living room of the cottage, Merry running beside her, begging for a walk. One she wouldn't be getting because Ben had made Raven promise she'd stay inside while he was gone. Too bad. Without a job, the days were long and empty, leaving her with too much time to sit and think.

She stared out the window at the fading light. She'd spent a lot of time praying and reading the Bible during the past few days, and still the chains that held her to the past were there. Knowing Shane, allowing him into her life had made her crave the kind of marriage Ben said he'd had. The kind she'd hoped to have with Jonas. The kind she still wasn't sure existed.

Ben's sedan pulled up in front of the house, distracting her from her thoughts. She watched him step out of the car. Evening sunlight touched his hair with gold and highlighted the broad expanse of his shoulders. He looked strong, confident and content, all the things Raven wanted to be and wasn't. As if sensing her gaze he glanced toward the window and smiled.

Raven hurried to the door and opened it, stepping out onto the porch. "Long day today."

"Visitation. I spent most of the afternoon at the hospital."

"How'd it go?"

"Two new babies to add to the congregation, and Mikey Samuels is recovering well from an emergency appendectomy. How was your day?"

Long. Boring. Frustrating. Raven refrained from saying so. "Good. Sam Riley stopped by for a few minutes. We're invited to dinner at his house after church next Sunday."

"He's got another puppy to give away?"

Raven laughed and shook her head. "No, but he mentioned a kitten."

"Better watch it. He'll have you owning a zoo before he's finished." He stepped to the back of the sedan as he spoke and opened the trunk. "I brought you something. Come help."

Raven hurried down the porch steps and peered into the trunk. There were several flats of plants inside, some flowered, some not, all with the pungent aroma of earth clinging to them.

"What's this?"

"Your new assignment." Ben lifted a flat and placed it in Raven's arms.

"Assignment?"

"Something for you to do tomorrow. All your pacing is starting to wear the floor down."

"I'm sorry. I didn't mean to be annoying." She carried the box to the porch and set it down on the floor.

"You weren't, but I can tell you're restless. This'll

burn off some of your energy." He slid a box down next to the one Raven had carried.

"I don't even know what any of these are."

"That's where these come in." He pulled a stack of books from the trunk.

"I've got a black thumb, Ben. These plants will be dead within a week." Despite her words, Raven was intrigued. She'd never had a flower garden. Now might be the perfect time to learn how to plant and care for one.

"You'll put as much effort into it as you do everything else and you'll end up with the most beautiful garden in Lakeview." He smiled and put another flat in her arms. "Now let's get these to the porch. I've got a meeting tonight."

They carried the plants to the porch and then stepped inside the house.

"I stopped by the Montgomery house to see how Abby's doing. She asked me to bring you something." He pulled a small leather book from his back pocket and handed it to Raven.

"What is it?"

"I don't know. Neither did Shane, but Abby was insistent that I give it to Thea. Shane said that's you."

Raven glanced at the cover, ran her fingers over the embossed words. "I think this might be the book Abby went into the garage for on the night of the fire. She was beside herself and insisted that we find it."

"Must mean something to her."

"I guess so. I just wish I knew what. How is Abby?"

"The same. A little vague. Forgets words. Not eating much. And asking for you."

"For Thea, you mean."

"No. For you. She might get confused, but she knows

you're a nurse. She's told everyone who cares to hear that you were the only person who hasn't tried to poison her. You need to go back."

"I know."

"Then do it."

"If it were just about Abby, I would."

"Abby won't be around forever, Rae. Now's the time to do what's right, no matter how scared you are of what doing it will bring. I've got to head out. Want to come?"

"No. You go without me. I'll be fine."

"You sure? You've been cooped up in the house all day. You must be getting antsy."

"A little, but I doubt crashing a meeting will cure me. Besides, I want to read this book, see if I can figure out why it's so important to Abby."

"See you later, then. Keep the doors locked."

"I will."

"It's supposed to storm tonight. You know where the flashlights and batteries are in case the electricity goes out?"

"Yes."

"The windows are closed and locked?"

"Yes." Raven rolled her eyes and shoved Ben toward the door. "Now go."

He chucked her under the chin and planted a kiss on her cheek, then walked to his car and waved as he got in. Before Raven could close the door, he was out again. "Almost forgot. I'm supposed to give this to you, as well." He walked back and handed her a small box wrapped in foil paper. "Gotta go."

Raven glanced at the box, curious to know what Abby had sent her, but wanting to wait for a while to open the box. The night was still young and she had hours to occupy before Ben returned. She waved as he drove away, then closed the door and locked it against whatever threat might be lurking beyond the cottage walls. The thought worried her, made her check the windows and doors twice before she carried the little book and the box upstairs where predatory eyes couldn't peer into the windows.

Silly. She knew it, but her nerves were on edge, her heart pounding a strange rhythm as a rumble of thunder broke the silence. The storm. The change in atmospheric pressure was making her jumpy. Raven tried to convince herself of that as she sat on Ben's bed and opened the book. But even as she read, even as she tried to find a clue as to why the book was so important, her mind shouted that something was coming—something more than a storm.

The book was interesting, but not enough so to keep her mind from churning. Raven turned a page, rubbing a foot against Merry's fur. She wondered why the non-fiction account of an eighteenth-century woman's life was so important to Abby.

"Maybe the box has something more interesting." She peeled back the foil wrap, lifted the lid. "It can't be." Her fingers trembled as she lifted the silver locket from its bed of cotton. Then she flipped open the clasp. *Micah.* Tiny baby features just formed and not quite the child he would have been.

Raven didn't know she was crying until tears dripped into the box and wet a piece of paper that had been folded beneath the locket. She pulled it out, wiping at tears with her other hand as she read.

A gallant knight never breaks a promise. I found this in a pawnshop in Richmond. The owner was holding it, not wanting to sell it because of the photo inside. God is good, isn't He? Jake says you can have it back. Your son is beautiful, by the way. Like his mother. We miss you. I miss you. Always, Shane.

Shane had kept his promise.

Despite Raven's unwillingness to trust him, despite the fact that she'd walked away from Abby and from him, he'd done what he said he would. He'd found the locket.

She sniffed and rubbed a hand against damp cheeks, barely seeing Micah's picture through her tears. Her life had been lacking in the kind of connections she'd longed for, bitterness eating at her soul. She'd thought herself alone, but now she saw the truth. God had been with her all along, guiding her to this place. A place of healing, a place where she'd found not just a brother's love, but friends, community, a sense of belonging. Home.

If she dared reach for it. If she dared trust in it.

More tears poured down her face and she let them come, praying for healing, praying for understanding, knowing this time she would have both—and with them the life God had wanted for her all along.

Thunder clapped and crashed, waking Shane from the light sleep he'd fallen into. He groaned, eased the kink from his neck and eyed the paragraph he'd been working on. Another dark-haired princess in a pale, flowing dress. He grimaced, hit delete and closed the laptop.

He'd tried, really tried, to get Raven out of his mind. He had thought he was succeeding. He'd been wrong. She'd jumped out of his head and into his manuscript.

Great.

He wanted to phone her, tell her she could come back to work and they'd go on the way they had before. But it wouldn't be right. He knew it, and he felt sure she did, as well. God had a plan. Shane wasn't sure what it was, but he did know the only thing that made sense was letting Raven have time and space to put the past behind her. Until she did, there could be no future.

"Mr. Montgomery?"

Abby's newest caregiver knocked on the open door, and Shane stood to face her. Tall, with a broad, plain face, Shannon O'Malley had proven kind and efficient. Though Abby hadn't bonded with her, Shane knew he could trust the woman. Especially since he'd double- and triple-checked her references.

"Is everything okay?"

"I'm not sure. Abby went into the bathroom a while ago. She hasn't come out yet."

"She might need some help with her clothes."

"I called to her. She didn't answer…and the key is missing. It's not hanging from the door like it's supposed to be."

Shane's heart jumped, but he stayed calm as he hurried down the stairs and knocked on the door.

"Abby? You okay?"

"Is there another key, Mr. Montgomery? Another way to open the door? I'm really worried."

So was he, but he didn't waste time saying so. Just ran to the kitchen, found the key ring with spare keys and raced back to the bathroom. His fingers fumbled as he tried to get the door unlocked.

"Abby?" he shouted as the door swung open.

The bathroom was empty, the window open. Rain

and wind slashed against Shane's face as he lunged across the room and peered out into the darkness. He could see nothing in the blackness.

He swung around, ready to lash out at the caregiver, but she was pale and shaken, the phone in her hand, held out for him to take.

"We need to call the police. She could be hurt or lost."

"How long was she in there?"

"Fifteen minutes. No longer."

"You're sure?"

"Yes."

Shane nodded, letting go of his anger, knowing it was useless. "I'm going out to look for her. You call the police. Ask them to contact Sheriff Reed. Once you've done that, call the names on the emergency contact sheet taped to the fridge."

He didn't wait for her to respond—just trusted that she'd do as he asked. He opened the front door and stepped out into the storm, hoping Abby had gone to the same place she'd gone so many times before.

Raven sniffed back the last of her tears and stood. Her body felt stiff, her eyes burned, but her heart was light and she smiled as she lifted the locket. She'd call Shane, thank him, tell him she was ready. Ready to work. Ready for whatever they might build together.

She was turning to grab the phone when Merry leaped to her feet and dashed toward the stairs, barking frantically. The sound of a fist banging against the front door followed, and Raven raced down the stairs, her heart hammering in her chest as she shouted through the door. "Who's there?"

"It's Shane."

She pulled the door open, thinking he had come about the locket, but saw his face and knew she was wrong. He was soaked, his hair plastered to his head, and he was gasping as if he'd run long and hard.

"What? What's wrong?"

"Have you seen Abby?"

"No."

"She climbed out the bathroom window. Maybe twenty minutes ago."

"Let me get my coat, I'll come search with you."

"No. She might be heading this way. If she is, I don't want the cottage to be empty when she gets here."

"I can't just wait here while she wanders around alone in the storm." Raven started toward the coat closet, but Shane grabbed her arm and pulled her back.

"It's not just Abby I'm worried about. What if someone else is wandering around in the storm? Someone who wants to finish what he started a few weeks ago."

"And what about Abby? That same person could be with her right now."

"I know that. The police are on their way. So are Mark and Adam. Stay here. Leave all the lights on. Make it an easy place for her to find."

They were wasting time arguing. The knowledge was in Shane's eyes and in Raven's heart. She nodded.

"Call me. As soon as you know anything."

"I will."

Then he leaned down and kissed her. The warmth of his lips made Raven long to tell him what she finally understood.

She didn't have a chance. He pulled back, his eyes blazing with everything he felt, then stepped outside and disappeared into the storm.

Raven shut the door against the rain, useless energy coursing through her. The house was eerily quiet, Merry silent and still, staring at the door as if sensing the danger that lurked on the other side. Raven scooped her up and ran through the house, turning on every light, flicking on the outside porch light and the one outside the laundry room door. She prayed Abby would see them, prayed she'd be drawn toward their welcoming glow.

Where could she have gone? And why? Another book hidden in some secret place? A special spot that was just hers? A childhood retreat that she was just now remembering?

The possibilities were endless, the list screaming through Raven's mind as she ran upstairs, flipped on the overhead light and moved the desk lamp close to the window. *Please, God, let her see it. Let her be coming to me. Let her be safe.*

Outside thunder crashed and rumbled, and the wind gusted against the sides of the cottage and rattled the shutters. The ground would be wet and muddy, the way difficult for a woman in Abby's condition. She could fall, be hurt, or worse. Yet even as these images rushed through Raven's mind, her prayers continued. God *could* save Abby from the storm. He *could* bring her safely home. She trusted that, believed it in a way she hadn't believed anything in a long time. The peace, the strength she'd longed for, finally hers…

Merry whined in her arms, squirming to get down, and Raven bent to release her. That's when she saw the book Abby had given her. It had fallen open on the floor, the spine buckled and pointing up, and there, edging out of the opening, was a piece of paper.

Her hands trembled as she eased the paper out and

unfolded the yellowed sheet. Words were scrawled across it, the ink smeared and faded. Still, names leaped out at Raven—*Daniel, Thea*. Names she'd heard many times since coming to Lakeview. She skimmed the letter, her heart pounding harder with each word, her mind barely able to grasp what she was reading.

My dearest Thea,
If only I could look you in the eye and tell you how sorry I am. If only I had a chance to go back and undo what I've done. It's too late, though. Too late to make different choices. Too many people would be hurt. Too many lives ruined.

God help me. How can I go on knowing that I've hidden my brother's crime? I tell myself that Adam is right, that it was an accident, that Daniel didn't mean to kill you, that you're dead, and that nothing I do now can change that. But is that the truth? I don't know. I only know that nothing can change what I've done. What we've done. I wanted to protect your memory. All I've done is hidden you forever. Even if God can forgive me, I'm not sure I can ever forgive myself.

The rest of the words were blurred and difficult to read. Raven didn't try. Her hands shook as she folded the letter and placed it inside the book. The truth would have to come out. She'd give the letter to Jake and he could decide what to do, but first they had to find Abby. Snippets of conversation ran through her mind, things Abby had said that only made sense in the context of what Raven had just learned. The cemetery. Abby had said she'd left Thea there, near a tree with two crosses.

Is that where Abby had gone?

She grabbed the phone, dialed the Montgomery house and got the answering machine. "Shane, I think I know where she is. Out on the cemetery hill. I'm going to find her."

Then she hung up the phone, grabbed a flashlight, pushed Merry away from the door as she opened it and ran out into the night.

Wind gusted around her as she raced up the driveway and onto the road. It was the longer way, but safer. There were lights in the distance, men and women checking the fields and the woods near the Montgomery house. No one was on the road. Had Shane thought of the cemetery? Raven could only hope he was already there, leading Abby home, away from the steep hill and the lake's turbulent water.

Thunder crashed, cracking through the night like a gunshot, and Raven ran faster, the knowledge of what had happened so many years ago spurring her on. It seemed inconceivable that Daniel Meade had murdered Thea, and even more difficult to believe that Abby had hidden the crime. But she had. Raven knew it as surely as she knew Abby was at the grave now, her need for atonement so strong it stayed with her even as the images of her life faded away.

Raven's feet slipped on mud and wet grass as she ran across the field and up the hill into the graveyard. She slowed, shining her light around the area, but saw no sign of Abby. The edges of the cemetery were dark and lined with trees, and there was no evidence of the crosses she sought.

She skirted the fence, pushing through thick overgrowth, feeling tree limbs and thorns tearing at her clothes. She'd almost given up hope when her flashlight illuminated a piece of cloth caught on a branch and swaying in the wind. She grabbed it, searching for other signs that Abby had been there and finding loose earth piled close to the trunk of the tree.

Raven bent down, looking for footprints, but the ground was soaked, water puddling near the base of the tree. She straightened, turned and saw what she'd been looking for. Two crosses carved into the wood of the old oak. Raven's heart skipped a beat. This was it, then. But where was Abby?

She pushed back through the thick brush and ran down the slope that led to the lake, praying she would find Abby there on the dock where she'd been the day they'd met. Thunder crashed around her and the wind whipped into a wild fury. Raven's foot slipped and she fell, sliding down the steep hill, losing her grip on the flashlight. Lightning flashed as she struggled to her feet, and she saw a figure on the dock, too tall to be Abby, but someone…Perhaps a searcher, looking for signs of the missing woman. The image was gone as quickly as the lightning. She opened her mouth to call out, but the wind tore the words from her lips.

She didn't try again—just ran the rest of the way down the slope, heedless of the rain and wind and mud. Another flash of lightning revealed an empty dock and, to the right, the figure she'd seen moved toward the Montgomery property. She planned to follow, but something pulled her toward the dock and the seething black water that surrounded it. Each flash of lightning brought her closer, until her feet pounded on slick wood.

Her heart raced in her chest as she slid to a stop at the edge of the dock. "Abby!" This time her voice flew out, strong, firm, carrying across the water and back to her. "Abby!"

Lightning slashed across the darkness of the lake, and there, just yards from the dock, a still, white figure floated in the water.

"Dear God!" The words were a prayer shouted into the wind as Raven dove into the water, grabbed Abby and turned her over, dragging her toward shore, where she carried her up onto dirt and grass.

"Breathe! Breathe!" She shouted the words as she pumped water from Abby's lungs, felt for a pulse. She found it, thready, weak, but there. Heard the first coughing gasp of Abby's breath.

It was only then that Raven realized she and Abby weren't alone. Someone stood beside her, a dark shadow, tall and thin in the gray night.

"She alive?"

Adam. The other half of the secret Abby had kept.

"Yes. We'll need to get help. It would be best for us to take her out on a backboard."

"That won't be necessary."

"We don't have a choice. Carrying her out might worsen any injuries she sustained."

"Like I said. It won't be necessary. Poor Aunt Abby didn't survive and I'm afraid you didn't, either."

Chapter Twenty

Fear made Raven cold and she shivered as she stood, putting herself between Abby's inert form and the man who should have been no threat, but seemed one.

"That isn't funny, Adam."

"Neither is your interference. This could have been over days ago if not for you."

"I don't know what you're talking about." She edged to the side, leading him away from Abby, desperately hoping someone would come.

"Don't act stupid. You know. Why else would you be here? Everyone else assumed Abby would be near the cottage—she's been so fixated on Thea lately. They're searching the woods and fields on both sides of the road. And here you are, just come from the cemetery. What did you find there, Raven? Anything interesting? Anything you might want to tell people about?"

"I thought Abby might visit Daniel's grave."

"You don't lie well, you know. Not that it matters. I can't let you go now. Abby has to die tonight, before someone else starts making connections. The sheriff's already questioning people about Thea's disappearance. Can you believe it? A black woman, gone thirty-five years, and he's nosing at the story, trying to find clues."

"Clues to what? She left town. Everyone knows that." Raven took another step back, leading him farther away from Abby as thunder again shook the world.

"You know what happened to Thea. I don't know how, but you do. And that makes you as dangerous to me as my dear, softhearted aunt."

"It was an accident, Adam. Your father didn't mean to kill Thea. What harm will it do for people to know what happened? For Thea to get a proper burial? For her family to have closure."

His laughter filled the air around them, vying with the storm for control of the night. "So Abby really believed me. I always wondered. Always worried that one day she'd realize how unlikely my story was and go to the police."

"What do you mean?" But Raven knew. Lightning flashed and she saw the evil in his eyes. She shuddered and took another step back, hoping to buy time.

"I mean, I should have killed her thirty-five years ago. Should have made it look like my father went crazy. Instead I let her live, afraid the police might see through my story. Abby was soft—she didn't want to hurt Thea's family or mine—but I always worried she'd crack under the pressure of keeping the secret. I was right."

"She didn't tell anyone."

"No, but she will. Even if it is just the ramblings of an old lady. I thought I'd have her put away somewhere, in a place where no one knew about Thea Trebain. Shane wouldn't hear of it. So I had no choice. It was Abby or me. You should have stayed out of it."

Suddenly he lunged for her, his shadow moving in the darkness, and then his hands were grasping her arms, tugging her forward, pulling her toward the lake.

She struggled and fought against his hold, twisting until he pulled her arm up behind her back.

"Stop fighting. It won't do any good. The end will be the same."

"You killed Thea, didn't you? That's why you're doing this."

He laughed again, the sound bitter and filled with hate. "That's the only part of the story that was true. Her death *was* an accident. I was home alone, Mom and my sisters gone for a week. Dad out on a walk. My bags were packed, ready for my trip back to college. Thea came to the door, said she needed to speak to my father. One look at her and I knew she was pregnant. Didn't take a genius to know whose baby it was. I told her to get out. She refused."

"So you shot her."

"I took out my father's gun, waved it around, threatened her. That would have been it, but she grabbed the gun. It went off. She was dead before she hit the floor. Next thing I knew Dad was in the room, screaming, accusing me of murder. He reached for the phone and I did what I had to do—put the gun up against his head and pulled the trigger."

"No."

"It was Dad's fault. He saw Thea at her mother's funeral and couldn't resist, started sneaking off to see her every few days. Not that I blame him. Mom was a cold fish. Still, can you imagine what people would have thought if Dad had done the right thing and acknowledged that baby?" He shoved Raven forward as he spoke, his hold still tight on her arm.

"You're crazy."

"I'm smart. No way was I going to pay for something my father caused. So I called Abby, told her Thea had planned to leave town, that Dad had threatened to kill himself if she did. Told her they'd struggled over the gun, that I'd run in just as the gun went off, that when Dad saw what he'd done, he killed himself. She bought it, hook, line and sinker."

"And you convinced her to help you hide what happened."

"Exactly. She loved them both too much to let their names be dragged through the mud. Worked out nicely. Until now."

They were on the dock, water seething on either side, rain slashing from the sky, making the wood slippery. Raven used it to her advantage and pretended to fall, twisting as Adam's grip loosened. She turned, shoving hard against his hold, hearing rather than seeing him go down. His fingers grazed her ankle, grasping for a hold as she leaped away, off the dock and into the churning water.

Streaks of lightning flashed across the sky, but it wasn't that Raven feared. Adam was up, a dark shadow leaping off the dock and into the water toward her. She dove below the surface and did the one thing she thought he wouldn't expect, swimming back toward the dock, grasping slick, wet wood and pulling herself up.

He'd seen her. She could hear his shouted curse. Then she was on the dock, feet flying, her one thought, *Abby.* A hundred yards. Fifty. She could see Abby's still form lying abandoned on the sandy ground.

"Abby! Get up! Run!"

Abby stirred, shifted, opened her eyes.

"Hurry!"

Something caught at Raven's hair, dragging her backward, and Adam was there, his teeth flashing white in the darkness.

"A hero's death for a wonderful and caring nurse. Dying in the line of duty. Seems fitting, don't you think?" He shouted the words above the sound of the storm, above the pounding of Raven's heart, and her terrified gasping.

She screamed, tried to loosen his hold as he dragged her back into the water and shoved her head beneath the surface. She forced herself to go limp, forced herself not to struggle. Her fingers brushed the bottom of the lake, searched the mud and muck, found something hard. She pulled it up, waited, her lungs burning, until the moment she knew would come, the moment Adam thought he'd won.

His hold relaxed, and she lunged, slamming the rock into his face. He howled and fell back, and she whirled away, water and mud trying to hold her back, screaming for Abby. She knew it was only a matter of time before Adam had her again. And then he was on her, slamming her onto the ground, dragging her backward.

Someone was screaming. Shane could hear the sound above the pounding storm around him. "You hear that?"

"What?" Jake paused, looked around at the gravestones. "All I hear is rain and thunder."

"Someone's screaming. I'm sure of it." The sound came again, this time louder, as if someone were racing toward them from the lake.

"Let's go!"

They ran down the hill, their lights illuminating the darkness, and then saw a figure, stumbling along the path. "It's Abby!"

All the worry, all the fear Shane had been carrying with him for the past hour disappeared. He sprinted forward, pulling her into a hug. "Abby, thank goodness, I've been worried sick. Let's get you home."

"No. He's got her. Hurry. *Hurry*."

And that's when Shane heard another scream.

He didn't stop to ask, didn't bother trying to think about what it meant. Just raced down the slope, sliding, slipping in the mud and grass, rain and wind beating at his face, stinging his eyes. Blinding him.

He heard a grunt, a muted scream, and then turned his light in the direction of the sounds. Two people were struggling near the edge of the lake. One larger, stronger, dragging the other into the water. The smaller figure, fighting, pushing with arms and legs—long, wet hair trailing into the black water.

Shane dropped the light and sprinted across the space that separated them, then pulled at the man, jerking him back from Raven, tackling him to the ground and holding him there.

"You got him?" Jake shouted through the darkness, his light bobbing close, then landing on the face of the man Shane held.

"Adam?"

His cousin bucked, tried to free himself, but he was years older and pounds lighter, and Shane held him still.

"You murdering—" Shane began.

"Cool it." Jake grabbed Shane's shoulder, urging him up. Then he pulled Adam to his feet. "Seems we've got some things to discuss, Mr. Meade."

"I want a lawyer."

"You'll get one. But let's make sure you know your rights first."

Shane didn't bother listening—just turned away and knelt on the sand near Raven, bracing her shoulders as she coughed lake water onto the ground. "Are you okay? Did he hurt you?"

"I—I'm fine. Where's Abby?" She gasped the words out, her teeth chattering, her body shaking so hard Shane didn't know how she'd managed to speak.

"I'm here."

And to Shane's surprise, Abby knelt beside Raven and put a frail arm around her waist.

"I'm here," she repeated.

"Oh, Abby. I was so worried."

"Why? Didn't you know the gallant knight would rescue us? That's the way it should always happen."

Raven's laughter was watery, but real, and Shane started to pull his hands away, knowing she'd be fine, knowing it was time to move away.

She caught his hand. "Don't go."

"I wasn't going to." And he settled back down, still holding her hand, knowing that everything he'd hoped for was encompassed in those two simple words.

"Everyone okay?" Jake's light bobbed across the ground.

"Looks like it." Shane stood and helped Raven and Abby to their feet, putting an arm around each.

"Good. I've got an ambulance coming just in case. Let's get back to the house. See if we can make head or tail of what's going on." He stepped past them, pulling Adam along.

Raven stumbled a little as Shane urged her forward. Her legs felt shaky, her body trembled, but it felt good to have his arm around her shoulders, guiding her as they moved up the hill.

As they crested the rise the sound of voices rose above the storm. She could see lights moving toward them, and shadowy figures rushing through the rain.

"Mom!" Mark appeared, his face illuminated by the flashlight he held, worry creasing his forehead as he pulled Abby into a hug. "Thank goodness you're okay."

"No thanks to Adam." Shane's arm tightened around Raven as he spoke, and she leaned her head against his chest, too tired to do more than listen.

"I know. Officer Marshal just brought word that they found Renee. She said she was paid to sedate Abby. That Adam brought her the pill, told her to make sure the alarm system wasn't set. He said he wanted to bring Abby outside, make it look like she was wandering again—that it was the only way to get Abby the care she obviously needed."

"It's more likely he wanted to take her outside, put her in the garage and make it look like she set fire to the place."

Raven shuddered at the thought, and Shane rubbed his hand up and down her arm.

"You're freezing. Come on, let's get back to the house. We can talk there."

Then, before she realized what he was going to do, he lifted her into his arms and began walking.

"Shane, put me down. I'm too heavy."

"You're light as a feather."

"I can walk. You don't have to carry me."

"Sure I do. It's in the job description."

"Gallant knight?"

"No, good friend. More…if you'll let me."

She shifted, looping her arms around his neck, enjoying the strength of his shoulders, the heat of his skin

Epilogue

"I'm telling you, this soup is poisoned."

"It isn't soup, Mom. It's mashed potatoes. And it isn't poisoned."

Raven smiled as she walked into the house and heard Mark's voice drifting down the hall.

She took off her coat, tapped snow off her boots and rubbed Merry behind her ears, calming the dog's happy dancing. "Where's Shane, girl? Still in his office? Or has he finally come up for air?"

Merry barked and raced toward the kitchen.

If he wasn't done, Shane should be finishing soon, and Raven was prepared. She lifted the grocery bags and headed for the kitchen.

The room was warm and bright, a welcome after the snowy grayness of the February day. Even more welcome were the people who filled the kitchen—not just Abby and Mark, but Ben and Shane. Raven smiled and stepped into the room.

"Looks like I'm late for the party."

"You're back. I've been waiting for hours." Shane

jumped up from his chair and hurried toward her, a grin on his face.

"Sorry. It was snowing, so everyone in Lakeview was buying groceries."

"Don't let him fool you, sis. I've been here for an hour and can tell you for sure that Shane walked in the door less than fifteen minutes ago." Ben pulled out a chair. "Sit down and eat. It's still warm."

"Cooking again, Ben? You'll spoil us." But she moved toward the table anyway and slid into the seat, placing the bags on the floor near her feet.

"Gives me someone to cook for besides myself. I've got to run—meeting tonight. I'll see you all Sunday." He kissed Abby's head and Raven's cheek before he left.

"What a nice young man."

"Yes, he is," Raven answered, but her attention was on Shane as he slid into the chair next to her.

"I finished. Finally."

"I knew it would be today."

"Did you? You're not just gorgeous, you're a mind reader."

"And bearer of gifts." She reached into the bag and pulled out two cartons of ice cream. "Chocolate for Abby. Butter pecan for you."

"Then it's time to celebrate. But first I need to talk to you. Out in the hall."

Something serious—Raven could tell by the hardness in his eyes. She stood and followed him into the hall. "What is it?"

"Jake called. Adam's appealing."

"That isn't a surprise."

"I know, but I wanted to tell you anyway."

Raven nodded, lost in thought. The discovery of

Thea's body. Her funeral. The press and media that had bled the story. Adam's trial and conviction. The hate and fire she'd seen in his eyes as she testified.

She shuddered and Shane wrapped his arms around her, speaking against her hair.

"He won't win."

"I hope not."

"He won't. The evidence is compelling even without your testimony and Renee's."

"I still worry."

"Don't. It's over. Adam's going to pay for what he did."

"You're right." Raven blinked back tears and pulled away. "So let's go have that ice cream."

"Not so fast." He tugged her toward him. "I've just defeated a giant. Slayed him with nothing more than a computer and ten fingers."

"You're amazing."

"I am, aren't I? But I didn't do it for glory or riches."

"No?"

"No. I did it for one reason and only one. To win the affection of a fair maiden. One with hair as soft as silk and eyes as blue as the summer sky. Gold and silver pale in comparison to her beauty." He bent to kiss her, a gentle touching of lips.

"If it isn't gold or silver you want, then what?" She threaded her fingers through his hair.

"A kiss to prove I've won her heart."

And he captured her lips again.

"Well, it's about time. I didn't think you'd ever get married."

Abby's voice pierced the moment and Shane pulled back with a sigh.

"Well, I did. Don't you remember? The candlelight?

The horse? The white carriage? You wore that pretty yellow dress."

"Was that your wedding, dear?"

"It was."

"Wonderful. And when is the baby due?"

"October." The words were out before Raven realized she was going to say them.

Shane laughed and tugged one of Raven's curls. "Now you've done it. We'll never hear the end of it. You know Aunt Abby never forgets things like this."

"How could I forget a baby? I'll have to make some little mittens for his feet." She walked back into the kitchen.

As soon as she disappeared from view, Shane looped his arms around Raven's waist, tugged her close and began kissing a path up her neck. "Guess we'll have to work hard to make your story come true. We wouldn't want Aunt Abby to be disappointed."

Raven slid her hands along his arms and up into his hair. "That sounds like fun, but Abby isn't going to be disappointed. I really am pregnant."

She knew the moment her words registered. Shane went completely still, then pulled back and looked into her eyes. "You are?"

"Yes. That's what took me so long. I visited the doctor before I went to the store. I didn't want to say anything until I was sure."

"Are those happy tears I see in your eyes? Or sad ones?" He ran a finger along her cheek and caught a tear that had escaped.

"Happy. How could they be anything else?"

"Good, I'd hate to have to challenge myself to a duel." His words were light, his gaze intent as he studied her face. "You sure you're okay?"

"Better than that." And it was true. "I love you, Shane."

"And I love you. God did something wonderful when He brought you to Lakeview. Not just bringing the two of us together, but making us a family—you, me, Abby, Mark and Laura, and Ben. And now a baby. A little girl who looks just like you—midnight-dark hair and summer-blue eyes."

"Or a boy with your green eyes and creative genius."

"One of each might be interesting."

Raven smiled, tears pricking at her eyes again as she thought of all the last year had brought—the love, the connection, the sense of belonging.

"Don't cry. You know I'm not good at handling tears."

Raven laughed, and hugged Shane tight. "I'll try not to soak your shirt. I promise."

"Good. Now, how about that ice cream?" And he tugged her into the kitchen and the warmth of home.

* * * * *

Dear Reader,

Life is filled with ups, downs, twists and turns. That's not a bad thing when you like roller coasters. But if you're like me and enjoy the more placid rides, sudden changes in direction can be disconcerting. A lost job, a lost love, illness or death in the family—when we experience those things, it can be hard to remember that God knows every bump and turn our lives will take and that He's with us through them all, steering us forward, urging us on, quietly whispering to our souls that everything will be all right.

Raven Stevenson's life is a roller-coaster ride, and she's ready for it to stop. That means taking a break from her job as a home health-care nurse and moving to Lakeview, Virginia, to reconnect with a brother she hasn't seen in twenty years. She hopes she'll have time to think and to reassess the direction her life has taken. Instead she gets pulled into the lives of Abby and Shane Montgomery—an elderly women suffering from dementia and the nephew who is determined to care for her. Together the three of them must confront the past and uncover a secret that just might destroy them all. Only in doing so can they learn the true meaning of God's grace and love for them.

I hope you enjoy taking part in their adventure. If you have the time, drop me a line. I can be reached by mail at 1121 Annapolis Road, PMB 244, Odenton, Maryland, 21113-1633. Or by e-mail at shirlee@shirleemccoy.com.

May God richly bless your life.

Shirlee McCoy

Take 2 inspirational love stories FREE!

PLUS get a FREE surprise gift!

Mail to Steeple Hill Reader Service™

In U.S.
3010 Walden Ave.
P.O. Box 1867
Buffalo, NY 14240-1867

In Canada
P.O. Box 609
Fort Erie, Ontario
L2A 5X3

YES! Please send me 2 free Love Inspired® novels and my free surprise gift. After receiving them, if I don't wish to receive anymore, I can return the shipping statement marked cancel. If I don't cancel, I will receive 4 brand-new novels every month, before they're available in stores! Bill me at the low price of $4.24 each in the U.S. and $4.74 each in Canada, plus 25¢ shipping and handling and applicable sales tax, if any*. That's the complete price and a savings of over 10% off the cover prices—quite a bargain! I understand that accepting the books and gift places me under no obligation ever to buy any books. I can always return a shipment and cancel at any time. Even if I never buy another book from Steeple Hill, the 2 free books and the surprise gift are mine to keep forever.

113 IDN DZ9M
313 IDN DZ9N

Name	(PLEASE PRINT)	
Address	Apt. No.	
City	State/Prov.	Zip/Postal Code

Not valid to current Love Inspired® subscribers.

Want to try two free books from another series?
Call 1-800-873-8635 or visit www.morefreebooks.com.